I0727551

TOTLANDIA

THE ONESIES - BOOK 1 (FALL)

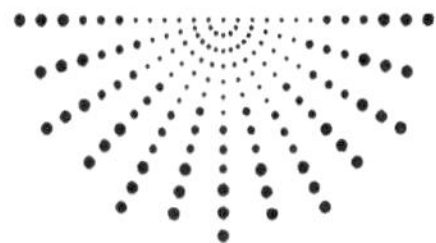

JOSIE BROWN

A BOOK BY

SIGNAL PRESS

ONE OF MANY GREAT SIGNAL PRESS BOOKS

San Francisco, CA

Library of Congress Cataloging-in-Publication Data is available upon request

Cover Design by Andrew Brown, ClickTwiceDesign.com

Trade Paperback ISBN: 978-1-942052-22-7

V022619

ground for half an hour and you'll realize moms can also be catty, competitive and incredibly judgmental. Josie Brown has that bunch nailed in her new book series *Totlandia.* Picture Desperate Housewives and *Sex and the City.* *Totlandia* would be the babies they'd create. The book is a blast, packed with humorous punches between these ladies whose very existence relies on their ability to keep up appearances. This author will have you howling as you devour this most recent work. Yeah, she's that good. And so are her books.

    —Stress Free, Baby

"Who knew that joining a mom and tot group would be so strife with maneuvers worthy of a presidential campaign? Membership in The Pacific Heights Moms & Tots Club supposedly can guarantee a bright future for your offspring. Although these women are mostly wealthy, there are a few that are just getting by. As the group opens up to new members, each mother has only one goal: to insure their child will have every advantage that money can and can't buy. I adored this quick read and can't wait to get further into the lives of these women. There are some really sweet moments mixed in with the catty wonderfulness that Brown always seems to capture. I just can't believe I have to wait until the installment which will be released soon."

    —Mary Jacobs, Bookhounds Reviews

CHAPTER ONE

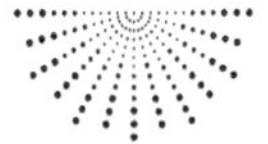

Labor Day
Monday, 3 September
10:37 a.m.

SINCE THE VERY FIRST MOMENT SHE HAD LAID EYES ON HIM, Lorna Connaught had loved Dante with a hot fierceness that both excited and shamed her.

The excitement came from the knowledge that, from then until the day she died, he would always be hers. Her shame came from the realization that she'd never felt such an achingly deep love like that before.

Not even for her husband, Matthew.

And yet, if it hadn't been for Matt, Dante wouldn't be in her life now.

She watched him as he warmed his feet in the sand. Alta Plaza Park crowned one of the highest peaks in San

Francisco's Pacific Heights neighborhood, affording marvelous views of the surrounding city. To the north, musky green Angel Island lay in the hazy turquoise bay. To the east was the mod white vertical square dome of St. Mary's Cathedral, backed by the city's skyscrapers. And from the south, the three candy-striped prongs of Sutro Tower pierced the cobalt blue sky. As on most days, the wind was brisk, whipping through the branches of the park's weeping willows and palms.

Lorna had come to realize that the park was just as much a haven for Dante as it was for her. Only here did he relax his usually rod-straight stance, so that his dark curls grazed his rounded shoulders.

Nothing made her happier than seeing him so content.

She breathed deeply, taking in the moment—

Taking in *something*.

What was that awful smell?

Oh, damn. Dante had crapped in his pants.

Lorna scooped up her one year-old son, slung his diaper bag over her shoulder, and headed for the nearest picnic table. She reached in the bag for Sensitive-Wipes, a changing mat, and a diaper. To her disappointment, there was only one in the bag. How typical of Matt to forget the one task she'd given him this morning: re-pack the diaper bag.

Well, one would have to do for now. In a few minutes, she and Dante were supposed to meet Matt at his mother's home for the family's annual Labor Day brunch. Eleanor Morrow Connaught, Lorna's mother-in-law, owned the largest mansion on the Jackson Street side of the park. While Lorna helped set the table, Matt could slip out to the store and pick up a few more since they were staying through dinner.

Dante was so antsy that it was hard for her to hold him and unfold the diaper at the same time. Frantically, she pulled off his pants, then removed the dirty nappy and cleaned his bottom with a wipe. She was about to grab the clean one when the wind whipped it out of her hand, where it hovered just out of reach, before floating over her head toward the playground.

"No! Oh, heck—" Running through the park in heels with a naked baby was not Lorna's style, but it was better than showing up at Eleanor's with her bare-bottomed grandson.

The diaper dipped and skipped in the cross-currents over the oblivious heads of the other mothers who sat on the benches all around the swing set. On holidays, the park was busier than usual, and this Labor Day was no exception. Lorna used her hands to shade her eyes from the sun's glare as she scanned the sky for the wayward diaper. She caught a glimpse of it sailing higher on the hill before plunging into a thicket of cypress trees.

By the time she got there, it was being wrapped around an 18-inch Journey Girls doll by two five-year-olds playing house.

The doll was laid out on an open paper napkin. Other dolls were propped up in a circle around her, as if watching a life-or-death medical procedure.

Lorna smiled down at the future mothers. "Your doll is very cute. What's her name?"

The little blond girl who had just patted one of the adhesive tabs in place over the naked doll's belly looked up at her warily. "Mewedith," she answered. Her lisp was the result of two missing front teeth.

"Yes, well, Meredith is quite pretty. But I think you've got my little boy's diaper."

"No, it's Mewedith's! See? It fits." The girl held up her doll.

Lorna kept her smile in place, but she shook her head firmly. "But you didn't bring it to the park. I did. I was putting it on my son when the wind took it out of my hand." She pointed to Dante. "Otherwise, he wouldn't be naked right now. So please give it back."

"No! I found it. It's mine now." The little girl frowned and grasped her doll tightly to her chest. The other little girl, thrilled at her friend's impudence toward an adult, moved behind her in solidarity.

"Excuse me?" Lorna couldn't believe her ears. "It belongs to my little boy. Hand it over. *Please.*" Her tone made it clear that it was not a request.

The girl shot her a bird. "Skwoo you."

What a little brat!

Cradling Dante in one arm, Lorna snatched the doll out of the girl's hands with the other. Both girls squealed as Lorna attempted to strip the doll of the diaper.

"Is something wrong here?"

The woman who confronted Lorna could have been

Brat's adult twin. An infant boy sat on her hip. He was around the same age as Dante, but unlike Lorna's son, he chattered and cooed as his arms waved in circles like little pinwheels.

The other little girl, who was now whimpering, ran over to the dark-haired woman who had accompanied Brat's mom.

"She wants to steal Mewedith!" Brat screamed.

"*What?* No! I'm not stealing anything." Lorna held up the diapered doll. "I'm just taking back what belongs to my son."

The woman frowned. "Are you trying to say that Meredith is your son's doll?"

"No, you don't get it. Your daughter has my son's *diaper.*"

The woman shook her head, confused. "I beg your pardon?"

"This diaper, on her doll, *it belongs to my son.* I was putting it on him when the wind blew it out of my hand. Your daughter picked it up before I could retrieve it."

The woman leaned down, nose-to-nose with her daughter. "Piper, honey, is that true?"

The little girl shook her head adamantly. "No, Mommy. It's mine."

The woman stood up straight. Turning back to Lorna, she shrugged with a smile. "I'm sorry, you must be wrong."

Lorna couldn't hide her shock. "Seriously? You're taking her word over mine?"

"My husband and I believe in positive parenting. We don't lie to her because it would set a bad example. At the same time, we trust her implicitly. If she says the diaper is hers, then it is."

"But of course it's my diaper! See?" Lorna held up Dante. "Why else would I be carrying a butt-naked baby?"

"I have no idea why people take naked babies out in public. Frankly, I find the habit disgusting and unsanitary." Unconsciously, her hand went to cover her tiny son's head, as if exposure to Dante might cause him to succumb to some deadly infection. "But I do know one thing: my daughter *never* lies. We trust her, and she trusts us."

"Then why don't you ask her where she got the diaper?"

"That's not the point. The point is that I believe her."

"No, 'the point' is that she's lying, and you're letting her get away with it because you'd prefer to pretend that your stupid parenting theory works."

Lorna was about to strip the diaper off the doll when Brat's Mom snatched it out of her hand. "Here you go, sweetie," she cooed to her daughter.

To hell with that.

Lorna grabbed hold of the doll by the hair. So her friend wouldn't lose the battle, Whimperer's Mother lunged for the dolls legs. Between the steely wills of the three women (not to mention their Pilates-toned arms) Meredith the Journey Girl didn't have a chance. When her head popped off, both little girls let loose blood-curdling screams.

"*Lorna?* What is going on?"

Lorna turned to find her sister-in-law, Bettina Connaught Cross, staring at her.

More to the point, she was staring at the savaged doll.

When her eyes moved to her nephew's naked butt, they opened even wider.

"Oh my God! Bettina…" The color drained from the faces of both Brat's and Whimperer's mothers. But instead of waving, they practically genuflected to Lorna's sister-in-law.

Lorna knew why. Bettina was the founder of the Pacific Heights Moms & Tots Club, the most exclusive playgroup in San Francisco.

When, finally, Bettina tore her eyes away from Dante, her gaze swept over the two women. "Janie! Coraline! Happy Labor Day! Lorna, Janie's little girl, Bailey, is in the PHM&T Fivesies group." She nodded toward Piper's friend. Then she smiled down at Piper, who also seemed awed by Bettina's presence.

Lorna thought it a bit much when Piper's mother nudged the girl into a curtsey. Bettina took it in stride, going so far as to pat Piper on the head.

"Ah, Piper. Such an adorable little girl. Janie, I presumed you mentioned to Coraline that the club just had an unexpected opening in the Fivesies. We're going to miss little Alistair Stewart-Putnam, but duty calls. The

British Consulate is transferring his father to Tokyo." She sighed deeply, as if the loss left her bereft.

Coraline nodded vigorously. "Yes, of course! I put in Piper's application the second I heard about it."

"Well…we shall see. Already the club's admissions committee has received twenty-eight applicants for the slot. Can you imagine? Of course, the Irish Consulate called immediately. He feels his niece should take it. But with his country's economic woes of late—granted, it's not her fault—but *still*. Personally, I've never bought into the philosophy of 'guilt by association,' but I'm just one vote among six—"

As if.

Like Lorna, Janie and Coraline knew that a kind word from Bettina went a long way with her fawning admissions committee.

"—her chances would have been better had six Lucas-Arts wives not also applied," Bettina continued. "Thank goodness Pixar is on the other side of the bridge, or we'd be inundated with their applications, too! Although, I must admit, PHM&T kids do love the invitations to all those free film screenings."

Coraline swallowed hard, probably realizing that the odds of her daughter's acceptance were in fact miniscule. As if cutting her losses on her eldest, she held up her squirming son to Bettina, like a fawning subject offering a gift to her queen. "I've submitted Ethan, too, for the Onesies group. His birthday was last Friday."

If she expected little Ethan to be kissed, it must have

been a terrible disappointment when Bettina backed away. "So robust, your little boy! He must be a handful. Well, here's hoping neither of their little hearts get broken." Her eyes widened at the thought. "On the bright side, I see you've both met my brother's wife, Lorna Connaught, and my little nephew, Dante—" Bettina smirked in annoyance "—who, unfortunately, seems to have lost his pants. What a messy little guy we have here! Lorna and Dante have also applied for a Onesie slot. Talk about a small world. Alas, there are six legacy families this year, so the odds are quite daunting for the four slots that are left. And one-hundred-and-three applicants!"

Janie and Coraline gawked at Lorna. In the few seconds it took for them to realize they'd been in a tug of war with Bettina's sister-in-law, their reddened faces had lost all color whatsoever.

For once, Lorna had a reason to be thankful in her sister-in-law's presence. "I was changing Dante when his clean diaper flew away. Little Piper found it."

Coraline pursed her lips. It was obvious to the others she was considering her next move in this most important game of social chess. If she didn't let go of the diaper, would she alienate Bettina and ruin her son's chances to get into the club?

Very slowly, she stripped the diaper off the doll and handed it to Lorna. "I'm so glad Piper was able to help."

Lorna shrugged. "Thanks. See you around."

The woman's eyes lit up, as if Lorna's goodbye might buy her a smidgen of goodwill with Bettina.

Lorna was tempted to warn her not to get her hopes too high.

For once, Coraline and Janie must have been thankful for Bettina's disdain of small talk, which allowed them to murmur their goodbyes immediately with the excuse that they, too, had somewhere else to be. They scurried toward the swing set, dragging their daughters with them.

"As if I'd ever allow *that* woman in the club," Bettina murmured under her breath. "What would that say about the club's sense of ethics?"

Lorna nodded. "I know! That daughter of hers, what a little brat."

"Silly. I'm not talking about the girl. It's her *father*. His IPO was an *enormous* disaster." Bettina waved her hand dismissively. "Speaking of scenarios that don't pass the sniff test, Lorna, I'd suggest you put Dante into his pants before we reach Mother's."

"Oh my God! I left them with his diaper bag, on the picnic table."

Bettina shook her head. "Run back and get it. I'll tell Mother I couldn't find you. She was miffed that Matthew let you take Dante to the park first."

There was no mistaking the edge to her voice. Bettina's four-year-old daughter, Lily, may have been Eleanor Morrow Connaught's first grandchild, but she wasn't her favorite.

That honor belonged to Dante, just as Matthew had been her favorite child.

I guess that's why Bettina hates me, Lorna thought.

Lorna got more than her fair share of Bettina's barbs, but the run-in with Janie and Coraline was a relief in one regard: it showed her that no one was spared.

Least of all anyone who gave a hoot about Bettina's club.

Lorna included. She needed it for Dante. In her eyes, he was perfect. Still, it dismayed her that, at fourteen months, he'd yet to take his first step. And he was so shy among other children, rarely looking at them. Not to mention he barely spoke.

Being in the club would give him more opportunities to socialize. But to get in, every vote in their favor would count. Especially Bettina's.

Lorna and Dante had just crested the hill when she spotted Janie and Coraline sitting on a bench right behind the table where she had left the diaper bag. It gave them a straight-on view of their daughters, who were now tossing themselves off the jungle gym onto a high pile of soft cedar chips that had yet to be spread by the park's maintenance crew.

"Ah hell!" Lorna overheard Coraline saying, "I guess Ethan's slot in the Onesies will go to Bettina's sister-in-law's mentally disabled nephew."

Dante—mentally disabled? How dare she!

Lorna was about to walk over to them and give them a piece of her mind, but then thought better of it. Getting into another ruckus with these women wouldn't prove anything.

They're just jealous of my sweet little guy. And the last thing I want them to think is that they've hit a nerve…but…

Could they be the right?

No, never. Not in a million years.

But, why didn't he smile more? Why wasn't he more attentive when she talked to him?

No. Dante was perfect. Those women were jealous. Their vicious cruelty toward Dante was proof of this.

Thank goodness Bettina had already made up her mind that Coraline's brood wasn't worthy of PHM&T.

And yet, Bettina always skirted any questions as to Dante's chances in the club. Surely she wouldn't let her feelings for Lorna get in the way of his membership.

Lorna couldn't ask her sister-in-law outright. The last thing she wanted was for Bettina to know she was worried about Dante for any reason. Bettina would have to feel the same about Dante as she did: that he was perfect. That he'd be an asset to the club.

She wrangled Dante into his pants, then started back up the hill.

She'd just arrived at the large wrought iron gates on Eleanor's estate when she realized Dante was wet again.

Frustration rimmed her eyes with tears.

She made sure to wipe them away before entering the corner grocery store, where the shop owners knew her as Eleanor's daughter-in-law.

Even there, appearances were everything.

11:14 a.m.

By their second mutual orgasm, Brady Pierce's latest lover had him convinced that the best lays were married women with toddlers whose husbands were workaholics.

"You know what they say," she whispered in his ear, "third time's the charm. You don't mind if I'm on top this time, do you?" Her grin was wide and naughty.

He cleared his throat. "Yeah, sure, be my guest."

A second later she was straddling him. She was still wet enough that she easily slid down onto him. With the practiced ease that comes with Bar Method-toned thighs, she inched up slowly, tightening around his member. Then back down…then up again…

Soon, this steady rhythm had her moaning ecstatically. Her eyes were shut tight, but he kept his open because he enjoyed watching the joy she showed in riding him. Had he been seventeen, just seeing her there poised over him, with that taut belly and those full breasts, would have had him coming again in no time. But he was a forty-two-year-old who had spent the last two decades of his life in front of a computer screen, and another decade before that on a couch, surfing too many TV channels and manipulating too many video game joysticks.

Sadly, their bouts of sex easily qualified as the most arduous workout he'd gotten in months.

At least in this position she could do all the work while he contemplated how to get what he really needed from her.

And it had nothing to do with his joystick.

Luck, nor fate, had anything to do with how they had met. He hadn't stalked her exactly, but he had been monitoring comments to and from the Pacific Heights Moms & Tots Club Twitter account (@PacHeightsMoms). She seemed to live online there. Quite frankly, he found that somewhat pitiful.

But since she was also one of the club's officers, she was perfect for his needs.

By the end of the week his short but charming posts had caught her attention. Her responses had been formal at first, then inquisitive. A month later, he showed up at Alta Plaza Park, one of the playgrounds she frequented with her children. He had recognized her from her online photo. Initiating small talk was easy as pie. He just plopped down beside her on one of the park's benches and pretended to be engrossed in some story on his iPad.

It took all of five minutes and one long low whistle to pique her interest as to what he was reading. He answered with the name of the classic, which he knew by following the club's Facebook fan page, was its book-of-the-month selection. *Voila!* A second later she was pontificating about its plot, characters, and still relevant social significance as if she'd written the damn thing herself.

The fact that his eyes never left her face as they discussed the book soon had her fiddling with her hair self-consciously. When he complimented her on the charm on her the necklace, she blushed. The reluctant wince she gave an hour later, as her kids pulled her off the bench demanding she make good on the fro-yo she'd promised them, left him no doubt that within a month's time she'd be sleeping with him.

Brady wondered how many times a week she'd taken her children to the park, hoping to bump into him again. He made sure it was infrequent enough to make her miss him.

When he did show up, he didn't exactly flirt with her. His style was to toss out a joke at his own expense, then wait for her to laugh, at which point he'd pay her a compliment, pointing out how well her kids played with their little pals, and how, when he first saw her, he thought she was an au pair because she looked much too young, not to mention toned, to be a mom.

That statement alone was catnip to her. It was the proof she longed for, that she was still attractive—perhaps even desirable—after having two kids.

It was also the day she started flirting with *him*. "If you give me your cell number, I'll text you proof of my stretch marks," she teased him.

He gave it to her and got back a full-frontal jpeg.

Not that he scrutinized it for any stretch marks. His appreciative gaze never went beyond her vajazzle.

In those early weeks it was obvious she never realized who he was, which was okay by him. Desired, in fact. Inevitably, she asked him which street he lived on. He replied that he lived at the corner of Baker and Beach.

That took her breath away. "You mean, across from the Palace of Fine Arts?"

He nodded. "I own that three-story Tuscan stucco. The one with the rooftop plaza."

Of course she would know the house. Maybe she didn't read *Wired* or *Fortune,* but he was sure she scrutinized every copy of *Architectural Digest,* especially the one six months ago in which Brady's house had graced the cover, since it was just down the hill from her own, in the Marina district.

That was the moment she realized he wasn't just some random guy named Brady, but Brady *Pierce,* the founder of BuyNowOrNever.com, last year's must-buy stock.

After that day, he had no doubt that part of her attraction to him was his notoriety. Still, it gave him pleasure to know that she had wanted him before she knew who he was, because it fell into his plan perfectly:

She'd have to believe that she had seduced *him.*

Granted, it was a strategic calculation on his part that she, like so many other stay-at-home moms, was truly lonely, despite a multitude of gal pals who were only a text away.

That the pregnancy glow, which had once warmed her marriage, had long since been scorched by the hot white realities of motherhood.

And that she was emotionally unfulfilled with her life, despite being freed from a nine-to-five tether.

Her savage eagerness during this very first tryst laid to rest any lingering doubts that she was also sexually frustrated, thanks to a husband who was either too busy or too tired to talk, let alone make love to her.

That was where Brady came in. He'd scratch her back if she scratched his. And yet, scratching was only part of their foreplay itinerary.

For him, sex was the appetizer. The main course was still to be had.

She's just like the heroine in that novel I read in some English Lit class, he thought. *Madame Bovary. She wants some guy—any guy—to notice her in some way—*

No, not just acknowledge her, but *love* her.

Why were all women so damn needy?

Needy, like Jade.

The thought of the wife he had dumped just eight months ago should have softened his boner. Instead, a tsunami of lust rushed through him—

Jade always did have that effect on him.

Good thing, too, because his Madame Bovary—or more appropriately, Madame Ovary—was also climaxing. This time, though, her moans were much louder. Brady must have been just as noisy because the next thing he knew the baby, who had been sleeping so soundly in the nursery, was now wailing.

They both froze mid-orgasm. Then, with a wistful sigh, Brady's lover eased herself off him. It wasn't that hard. A one-year-old's cry could make any man go limp.

Especially when the kid was his.

Brady didn't even bother to put on his boxer briefs as he stumbled out of his bedroom and into Oliver's. His son would learn about modesty soon enough.

Or maybe not, considering his mother had been a pole dancer.

Brady took the bottle out of its warmer, shook it, then tested it on his arm before putting it in front of his son. The bottle had barely touched Oliver's lips before the tot was sucking away at it, noisily.

To Brady, it was the most beautiful sound in the world.

He didn't know how long she'd been standing there watching them. It startled him when he heard her whisper, "My God, he's so adorable!"

Her nakedness had a bigger effect on his son than on him. Maybe if he hadn't been cradling Oliver at eye-level with her left nipple, the little guy wouldn't have reached out to her, declaring "Mama."

She laughed, and then ducked her head, embarrassed. "Thank goodness your wife expressed enough milk to cover him while she's away at her mother's."

Brady shrugged. No way in hell was he going to tell her the baby had never been near Jade's cosmetically inflated tits. Oliver had been on Enfamil up until two months ago.

Nor was he going to mention that Jade was long gone from their lives. Brady had the annulment pay-off receipt to prove it.

Not that Madame Ovary needed to know that. From the comments made on the club's Facebook page, it was clear that single parents were *persona non grata*. If she learned that Jade was out of the picture, she wouldn't be able to help Oliver at all, and his plan would fail.

Failure was not an option. The most important thing Brady Pierce had learned on his long and arduous climb to the pinnacle of the business world was that surrounding yourself with winners was the way you became one yourself.

Which was why, as crazy as it sounded, the Pacific Heights Moms & Tots Club was the first baby step on Oliver's journey to success.

The winning combination was brains, ambition, *and* money. A full bank account couldn't do it alone. Sure, his money could buy his son's way into Harvard or MIT or Stanford. But what good would that do if the kid wasn't motivated to learn? Before he'd dropped out himself, he had met too many guys on campus with more money than brains.

And as for having the smarts to make it once you were there, the high tech field was teeming with college dropouts who, like Brady, had willed themselves into billionaires. He'd be the first to tell you that it was a lot easier if you started with a stash of cash.

The ambition quotient was where PHM&T came in. Membership in the club would fast-track Oliver into the best private schools in the city, where he'd be challenged and learn to excel, all the way to Stanford. All the way to his owning a company on NASDAQ: something he'd start with his personal trust fund.

To ensure his son was this triple threat, Brady had sold his company and had become a stay-at-home dad.

It was why he had separated from Jade the minute he

realized she could never be the kind of mother Oliver deserved.

And it was why he was sleeping with this all too desperate housewife.

Sure, the sex was great. But it was only a means to an end. Madame Ovary held the key to Oliver's success. She sat on the acceptance committee of the PHM&T.

Time to get serious. He shifted Oliver toward her. "I can tell he's just as head over heels about you as I am. Why not make his day and hold him?"

She rocked Oliver in her arms. As he sucked on his bottle, he stared longingly at the nipple—the left one again. So near, yet so far.

Tell me about it, guy, Brady thought. *Just like your future.*

He looked Madame Ovary in the eye as he flashed his patented winner's smile. He would not blink. He had learned that trick years ago from his mentor, Steve Jobs, sometime during his first year at Apple: *Stare directly at the target until they are mesmerized. Then give them the directive, the grand mission, only they can carry out.*

Only this time the mission wasn't some computer, or the latest iPhone. It was Oliver's future. "You're going to pull this off for him, aren't you, sweetheart?"

She dropped her gaze to Oliver, whose eyelids fluttered as he drifted back off into sleep. "Oh honey, you know you can count on me."

Had she been addressing him, or Oliver? Not that it mattered. When it came to the welfare of his son, Oliver and Brady were one and the same.

Always and forever.

"How can you be so sure?" he asked. "You're only one vote on the committee. What about the other five members?"

The finger that had been stroking Oliver's cheek now silenced Brady's lips. "You're just going to have to trust me." Her laugh was anything but modest. "I know those women on the committee better than anyone."

Mission accomplished.

With what he hoped was just enough jealousy in his voice, Brady muttered, "Aw hell! Didn't you say you had to meet your husband and your kids at some picnic by noon? It's almost eleven-thirty."

The color drained from her face. "Oh my God. I've got to get out of here!" She pecked his cheek, handed over Oliver, and then hightailed it back into his bedroom.

He could hear her scurrying around. Rocking Oliver in his arms, he watched from the doorway as she snapped on her bra and then shoved her silk tee shirt over her head. "Damn it, I can't find my panties—"

He shrugged. "Go commando. No one will ever know." Least of all her husband.

The sap.

She shook her head as she yanked the bed sheets from one side to the other. "Are you crazy? What if your wife finds them?"

"She won't. She's out of town, remember?" Seeing the concern in his lover's face, he forced a smile and added,

"Seriously, don't worry. I'll hold on to them for you. Besides, it will give you a reason to drop by again."

She rose from under the bed, waving a hot pink thong triumphantly over her head. "Found it!" Slipping them on over her hips, she added, "But I can lose it again—I mean, if you think I need an excuse to come by."

"Never," Brady assured her. "Hey, just think: if Oliver gets accepted, we'll get to see a lot more of each other. You know, at club meet-ups and all."

"Quit worrying. He's as good as in." She winked knowingly as she zipped her jeans. "Him, and of course Jade. Ha! I don't know if I'll be able to keep from clawing her eyes out. I'm already pea green with envy. But I'm the least of her worries. Some of those women are real bitches."

Oh.

Fuck.

A pole-dancing bimbo taking play dates with a bunch of Pacific Heights yummy mommies? That is *not* gonna happen.

"With all her charity work I don't know if Jade will be able to, you know, hang out all the time. *Any* time, really." He chuckled to cover up his shaky voice. He prayed he didn't sound as desperate as he felt. "But, hey, what about me? I'm Oliver's wingman. He's why I sold my company in the first place. I never wanted to be one of those dads who are never around for all those impor-tant things in their kids' lives. I'm going to coach his Little League team, and his CYO Basketball. Hell, I'm going on every school field trip and joining the PTA, too. But it all starts with PHM&T, right? Babe, I know you can make that happen." He gave her a soulful kiss. "When we're in public I'll be on my best behavior. Scout's honor."

She shook her head playfully. "Silly boy! It's a *'moms and tots'* club, remember? There is one ironclad rule: *no dads allowed.*" Then she lifted up onto her tiptoes so she could kiss his chin. "Maybe it's for the best. Some of those women are terrible flirts. I'd be *soooo* jealous."

In other words it was Jade, not Brady, who held Oliver's golden ticket into the club.

Brady winced at the thought that his son's future was predicated on the actions of the ditz he'd just dumped.

He'd have to count on Jade doing the right thing.

For Oliver.

And if not for their son, then for the money Brady would pay her to act like a good mother for three mornings a week. It would cost him another fortune.

The second Madame Ovary slammed the door, Brady reached for his cell phone. He clicked through the J's, then remembered he'd erased Jade's number after the incident —the one where their son had almost died because she'd left him with her clueless manager while Oliver was sick with a high fever—just so she could audition for some low-budget indie film.

Brady had almost tossed Jade out the third-story window of the Pediatric Intensive Care Unit when she let it slip that the audition was for a porn flick. The only thing that saved her life was that she swore to him she had turned it down.

That was the moment he knew he could never trust her with his son, ever again.

It was also the moment he knew he had a choice: be the hottest internet entrepreneur on the planet, or the best dad in the world. If it meant calling Jade and asking—no, *demanding*—she do right by Oliver, then so be it.

It surprised him that he still remembered Jade's number.

It didn't shock him at all that it was disconnected.

That's okay. Within an hour, someone from his private security detail would find her for him.

The thought of her still made him ache, for all the wrong reasons.

1:24 p.m.

"Ah, my boy! My perfect, sweet little boy! Where have you been all my life?"

This inevitable declaration by Eleanor Morrow Connaught never failed to draw a hearty laugh from her son, Matthew, despite the fact that she wasn't addressing him but her grandson, Dante. It happened whenever the little boy came into view, whether it was the first time that day or like now, after he'd been roused from his nap.

Lorna's reaction to it never changed, either: she swelled with pride, knowing that after eight years of trying so desperately, it was Dante who had finally secured for her the respect she sought from Matthew's mother.

Matt propelled his son around the room with stiffened arms that went straight out in front of his chest. The softest landing Dante could make was always in his grandmother's arms, where he responded to the physical and emotional warmth he found there with a gentle smile.

Bettina's reaction was less indulgent. "Matthew, one day you're going to drop that boy, and all hell will break loose."

Matt shrugged. Bettina's acerbic barbs never seemed to prick her brother's perennially upbeat mood. "He'll bounce…right?"

Only Art Cross, Matt's brother-in-law, laughed at the joke that brought a chorus of groans from all the women.

"Mother, admit it: I was dropped on my head at least once, and it didn't hurt me."

"The jury is still out on that, Matthew." Eleanor's remark was accompanied with a raised brow.

Only Lorna seemed concerned that Eleanor's jibe was more than a joke at his expense.

Why am I concerned, Lorna chided herself. In Eleanor's eyes Matthew is perfect because he's her son. I feel the same way about Dante.

Watching her mother-in-law with her child, it was nice to know Eleanor did, too.

Just then, Bettina piped up. "Speaking of your perfect grand*children*, I got a letter from Lily on Friday—in *Russ-*

ian! Isn't it wonderful that she's also picking up a language while she's away at ballet camp?"

"Who?" Eleanor asked, as she tousled Dante's curls.

Bettina scowled. "Lily! My daughter. *Your grand-daughter.*"

Eleanor shrugged. "I was teasing, Bettina. Jesus, lighten up! It's just my way of letting you know how disappointed I am that you let her go away to camp for the whole summer."

"I can't help that they insist the dancers stay for ninety days. You know the Russians: such taskmasters."

"Lily is only four, Bettina. She is not a ballerina. She's a kid who wants to wear a tutu and pretend she's a fairy. She shouldn't be in St. Petersburg, Russia, but here with us."

"Mother, you were a ballerina. You know the dedication it takes. I'm sure Lily's drive and love of the art comes from you, and it is truly awe-inspiring—"

"Her drive, or yours, Bettina?" Eleanor looked over at her daughter. "Honey, I danced to meet and marry a wealthy man. And because I did, you and Lily don't have to. End of story." Eleanor sighed. "By the way, Lorna, that salad of yours…what was it again?"

"Quinoa and asparagus. I found the recipe online."

"Loved it. New and refreshing." She graced Lorna with a smile.

"I stuffed myself with Bettina's potato salad," Art piped up. Bettina rolled her eyes at him. If Art had been hoping his cheerleading would please his wife, he was wrong. Time to double down. "You liked it, too, didn't you, Mother Connaught?"

"Delicious," Eleanor declared. Bettina's shoulders eased with the compliment, but tensed again when Eleanor added, "Whole Foods, I presume?"

"No, Mother, I made it fresh! Yukon Gold potatoes, dill, and mustard seed, all from my own garden! And crème fraiche—"

"Did you curdle the cream, too?" Matt's question was posed seriously enough that Bettina paused before answering.

"My God, children. We're talking about potato salad. Give it a break." Eleanor shook her head sadly. "Is there anything for dessert?"

"Devil's food cake," Lorna responded at the exact same time Bettina said, "Lemon sorbet."

They stared at each other, then said in unison, "I made it myself."

Eleanor laughed out loud. "Aren't we busy little bees. Well don't just stand there, let's have at it."

"Let the games begin," Matt muttered, as both his wife and his sister moved toward the kitchen.

Lorna couldn't blame him for grumbling. He hated the way she and Bettina had turned every family gathering into a competition.

He can't really blame me for it, she reasoned. I wasn't the one who started it. But one thing is sure: I'm certainly not going to let Bettina act as if she is better than me, either as a cook or as a parent.

Besides, a little healthy competition never hurt anyone.

The sooner Dante learned that, the better.

At least Bettina waited until the coffee was served, and the cake was cut, before easing the most important issue of *Parents* magazine out of her tote bag and onto Eleanor's gleaming mahogany dining room table:

The one devoted to ranking "The Top 100 Moms-and-Tots Clubs in the US."

Bettina's attempt at humility was laughable at best. "I suppose I should be flattered that they chose Pacific Heights as the number one club in the country," she murmured with a sigh.

Matt grabbed it off the table. "Oh yeah? Based on what criteria? Which mom can send their kid to the most far-flung camp?"

"Don't be silly." Bettina sniffed. "Yes, youth trips are one criterion. And granted, we topped it. But the true reason we're first is because we rank highest in so many categories. For example, we're also number one in applicants who get accepted into our city's highest-achieving private schools. And we're number one in parents who are renowned—"

Matt nodded vigorously. "Oh, so they *do* include CEO and SEC perp walkers. Bravo, Sis."

Upon hearing that, Art's lavender complexion, which

had been attributable to the amount of Johnny Walker Blue he'd been guzzling since before noon, darkened to an aubergine hue. "Now see here, Matt. You and I both know that a lot of great men take the fall in the name of commerce—"

"Maybe not enough," Eleanor murmured.

All conversation ceased. Art's face went from eggplant to cauliflower. Last year, a financial investment he had made on behalf of Eleanor, in order to shore up his sagging partnership at Lichman Parker Bowles, had tanked—big time.

At the time, Eleanor had dismissed it by pointing out that, "It's exactly the amount I had set aside in Bettina's trust. Consider it a wash, Art."

Bettina realized it was time to change the subject. "There is one disappointment to being first in the nation. Seeing that the club has got such an incredible wait list already, all this can do is make it worse! Seriously, too many people consider themselves high achievers."

"Amen," Matt said as he wiped a chocolate smear from Dante's cheek. "What this country needs is a reality check. In fact, Bettina, you should make that the new mission of your club. Instead of playing zookeeper to a pack of tiger moms, think of what joy you'd have whipping all the clueless moms into shape! Sort of a mommy dominatrix. I guess that would make you a Mama-matrix, right?"

Even Art, Bettina's ever-faithful lapdog, snickered at that.

Bettina raised her head high. "The last people I'll let into the club are those who aren't accomplished."

Matt turned to face her. "What are you saying? It's a matter of 'My bling is heavier than your bling?'"

Bettina smiled. "Something like that. Or 'My title is heavier than yours.' And 'My bank account is larger,' or 'My credentials are better.' Status is what drives western society. It always has, and it always will. It's survival of the fittest. Everyone knows that."

Eleanor waved away that thought as if it were a bothersome gnat. "Bettina, you're not running some presidential cabinet. We're talking about kids who poop in their pants and the mothers who wipe their butts."

"And over a hundred of those mothers want to belong to the Pacific Heights Moms and Tots Club. They covet acceptance because it's the very first step their child will take on the road to success. In our club they, and their children, meet the right friends and make lifelong connections. They feed into the best preschools, elementary, and prep schools. They get a reference to Harvard or Princeton or Stanford, or a job at Microsoft or Apple or Google. They don't just survive, they thrive." She took Dante from her mother and leaned him against her hip. "Mother, you did it, too. You just said so."

Eleanor laughed uneasily. "Yes, I guess eventually I joined some mother's group and made a few friends. But what I said was that I married well."

"My point exactly. Even in this day and age, it all begins with the gold ring." Her gazed shifted to Lorna.

"But that's just the starting point. The club can afford to be picky. If you want in, you and your child have to earn the right to be there, no matter how well you've married."

I hear you loud and clear, Lorna thought. Yeah, okay then: Bring. It. On.

CHAPTER TWO

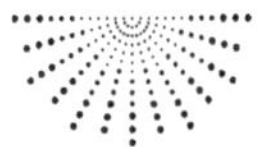

Tuesday, 4 September

ON PAPER AT LEAST, PROSPECTIVE MOM NUMBER 103 looked like a shoo-in to the Pacific Heights Moms & Tots Club application committee.

Attached to her application were four very enthusiastic endorsements, all handwritten, from current members (one each from the incoming Twosies-, Threesies-, Foursies-, and Fivesies groups).

And when grilled in the ensuing weeks by Bettina, these supporters hadn't revealed anything that could have knocked her out of contention: no bad habits or annoying tics, and no driving desire to get back into the workplace anytime soon.

Best of all, her husband had a real job: he was a financial manager at Schwab. Bettina winced whenever an applicant listed "self-employed" as her spouse's employment status, or worse yet "freelance." In the few short years Pacific Heights had been in existence, she'd learned that just meant these members would, at the very least, dominate their playgroup's conversation with the trials and tribulations of their teeter-tottering finances. More than likely the entrepreneurship would flounder, and the family would (a) move out of the city to a less expensive exurb in the Bay Area, like Santa Rosa (or worse yet, Tracy); or (b) the wife would have to go back to work anyway.

As for the working moms who slipped into the Club somehow, they weren't discouraged, *per se*, but politely ignored. And woe be it if they dared to send the au pair in their stead. The next time the execu-mom showed up, Bettina's stare was enough to make her shiver.

Eventually, they took the hint and quit coming altogether.

On the surface, Bettina's reason for encouraging the freeze seemed justified. "It's perfectly understandable that some mommies may have more important things to do. After all, there are only seven days in a week. Still, if you're not willing to devote three mornings to PHM&T, you'll never get the full benefit of our friendships—not to mention, you'll miss out on all the fun. That wouldn't be fair to you, let alone your poor child."

Like Bobbleheads, the members of Bettina's hand-chosen "Top Moms Application Committee"— Sally Dunder of the Twosies group, Mallory Wickett of the

Threesies, Kimberley Savitch of the Foursies, and Joanna Blunt of the Fivesies—nodded in unison.

Just as they were doing now.

But only because the committee was anxious to go ahead and vote.

Every morning for the past four weeks they had commandeered the Program Room in the basement of Pacific Heights' Golden Gate Valley Library to winnow down this year's Onesies group of one hundred-and-three applicants to a manageable number of finalists.

Now that they were down to the very last candidate, they were ready to get the hell out of there. They were bone tired and longed to take an aspirin—downed with a martini or two—to alleviate the month-long headache they'd endured at the behest of their peerless leader.

Bettina smiled supremely. She reveled in her ability to make others jump through hoops to the point of exhaustion.

"Let's see her in action, shall we?" she said, and clicked on 103's digital video file, which was already on the media screen on her iPad.

Nothing looked out of place. The woman's daughter, whose first birthday had taken place just last month, giggled sweetly in 103's arms. The bright stripes of the baby's long-sleeved Zutano jumper popped against 103's simple white shirt, which was buttoned up just far enough to expose the white lace camisole underneath. Rolled up at the sleeves and tucked neatly into her size two rag & bone denim leggings, it was a nice contrast to her husband's crew-neck black tee and relaxed-fit jeans: the weekend uniform of practically every thirty-something family man in San Francisco.

"Hi, I'm Heather," said the woman, smiling. As she held her baby to the camera, she added, "And this is Lola! We look forward to having fun with all the wonderful Pacific Heights moms and tots, don't we honey?"

The baby cooed and gurgled, as if on cue.

Before plucking the baby out of her arms, 103's hubby leaned over and gave his wife a swift kiss on the lips.

"Awwww." Sally sighed. "So adorable!"

Bettina rolled her eyes. By now she'd come to expect Sally's happy-pappy comments: the precursor to a thumbs-up for each and every applicant.

On the other hand, if Mallory didn't know them personally—and had therefore already divulged their flaws loudly and proudly—she could be counted on to take issue with some portion of their submission materials.

Like now. Mallory jumped up and pointed to the screen. "Oh. My. God! She is so *totally* disqualified!"

Kimberley and Joanna's desperate groans were loud enough to make Sally's two-year-old son, Linus, whimper in his sleep.

Sally frowned as she picked him up and rocked him gently. "Why, pray tell?"

"Rewind! Go ahead… Stop! Look…there, in the mirror, behind them. *You can see the person filming them.* He's using a semi-shoulder mount camcorder." Mallory jabbed a mauve-lacquered finger at the screen. "And if you're wondering why 103's family has such a beautiful glow around them, it's because there's another guy, off camera, holding up a lighting umbrella."

She was right. He, too, could be seen in the mirror.

"They've had this 'home video' professionally filmed. And that is against PHM&T rules, which clearly state, and I quote, 'photos or videos attached herewith must be representative of the applicant's true home life,' unquote."

Mallory's smile said it all: *gotcha.*

"Well, at least she's not fat," Sally muttered.

Bettina shot her a dirty look. No one dared to say it, but the proof was in the photos of more than half of the rejected applicants. If you were out-and-out fat, forget about it. Even applicants just a few pounds overweight weren't allowed in the club. In fact, the club's very few size eights raised eyebrows.

Especially if they dared to show up at the park in a racerback tank and Lululemon crops, toting a frozen latte.

It was enough to provoke Bettina to mutter under her breath, "She must own stock in Starbucks. Why else would she feel the need to increase its profits?"

As for Number 103, there was no getting around the fact that yes, she'd broken club rules. Bettina sighed loudly. "Well thank God she's the last applicant under review! Kimberley, how many finalists do we have to vote on?"

Kimberley took the now very slim "Preferred" folder and counted the applications still in there. "Of the twelve

Onesies slots, eight are already taken by legacy siblings. That leaves six applicants for the final four."

Bettina spread each qualified application face up on the table. "Just to refresh everyone's memories as to the finalists, the first one is Jade Pierce. She has a son, Oliver. The husband's name is Brady—"

"Oh my God! Brady Pierce?" Joanna murmured. "How hot is that?"

Mallory looked up with a smirk. "Who the hell is he? Not another rocker dad, I hope. Haven't we filled our quota on those?"

She was right. Seeing how this was San Francisco, there would always be a glut of musicians' families to choose from. Well, at least you could count on a rocker's baby mama to be svelte. Heroin chic and cocaine ass were much more desirable looks than thunder thighs and new mommy muffin top.

Kimberley's right brow shot up. "You've heard of BuyNowOrNever.com, right? You know, the deal-of-the-day website that just sold for like, a bazillion dollars? He's *the founder!*"

In response to Linus' hungry murmur, Sally released her right breast from her blouse. "That's good, isn't it? I mean, he's got to have some wonderful connections. Hey, maybe club members will be eligible for special discounts."

Mallory sighed. "Duh, silly. The products are already discounted. That's the whole point of the website."

Sally winced, more likely from Mallory's jibe than Linus' teething. "Who else is there?"

Bettina picked up the next application. "Ally Thornton cofounded Foot Fetish, the online shoe retailer, before selling it—for a tidy profit, I might add—and stepping out to have a baby. She's married to an attorney—Barry Simon—who works at Sillwick & Brest. Their daughter's name is Zoe." She held up the picture that came with the application.

Mallory frowned. "I don't know. It says here that she still sits on the company's board."

Joanna grabbed it and scanned it. "You didn't finish the sentence: '...in an advisory capacity.'" She shrugged. "What's the big deal? We all sit on boards."

Mallory shook her head. "Charities are different. Besides, those former career types can be such bossy know-it-alls!"

The others exchanged glances. "Talk about the pot calling the kettle black," Kimberley muttered.

"Well, she's got one thing going for her: she states her favorite charity is the San Francisco Ballet. I remember seeing her name in the program." Joanna tapped her cell. "Yep, it lists her in the Chairman's Circle, in fact."

The others took note of Bettina's appreciative nod. Her mother had been a ballerina, and it was one of the Connaughts' favorite charities as well.

In other words, case closed.

"Let's move on to the next candidate, Jillian Frederick," Bettina said. "Her husband is a partner in the international division of Colby and Trask Financial Managers—and he is a graduate of both University High and Stanford. He did his graduate work at Columbia. They have twin girls, Amelia and Addison."

"But if we say yes, we give up two slots." Kimberley's reminder sounded ominous.

Bettina was quick to counter with a smile. "Not to worry. Seems that what we've got left leaves us top-heavy with boys."

The sighs all around were genuine. No one wanted to break out that doorstop of a rejection file yet again.

"But accepting twins…won't that set a precedent?" Like a dog with a bone, Mallory couldn't let go of any apparent problem.

"It hasn't in the past," Joanna reminded her. "We've got the Bentley twins in the Foursies."

Mallory frowned. "But they were one of each, a boy and a girl."

Bettina's hand on Mallory's forearm was gentle but firm. "Things always have a way of working out."

In other words: *It's a foregone conclusion, so shut the fuck up.*

Mallory started to speak, but then thought better of it.

"Fine," Bettina continued. "That brings us to Lorna Connaught. Her husband is Matthew, and her son is Dante. She's on the San Francisco Foundation board and volunteers at Glide Memorial—"

"She's also your brother's wife, isn't that right?" Mallory's words sliced the air like a saber.

The other women hid their smiles as best they could. *Touché.*

Bettina waited a full sixty seconds before acknowledging the accusation. By the time she did, her lips were once again pursed into a stony smile. "Everyone here knows me well enough to presume I'd never play favorites. Lorna's good name and deeds stand on their own merits. In fact, I'll recuse myself from voting on her. If you pass on Dante, their little family will certainly be disappointed, but they'll weather it in stride. That is the Connaught way. Our tribe are hearty folk."

The other committee members exchanged anxious glances. Apparently none of them could cipher her true feelings about Lorna Connaught. Was Bettina's recusal some form of admission that she couldn't stand her sister-in-law? But wasn't that bit about "good name and deeds" her way of indicating they'd be fools to vote against Lorna, who also carried the Connaught name?

Not to mention that she had called the Connaughts a tribe. Did that mean they had Native American blood flowing through their veins? If so, and the committee voted them down, would they be branded as racists?

It was all terribly disconcerting.

Fuck the aspirin. Bring on the martini shaker. No glass needed.

Having successfully heightened their fear factor, Bettina's lips curled into a smile. "There is also Chakra Crutch. Stone, her husband, is a professor at Berkeley. Their son's name is Quest. Chakra has even offered to head up the club's organic vegetable garden."

Sally gave a loud sigh of relief. "Thank God! I've been saddled with that committee since my little Lucy was a Onesie! Well then, the woman certainly has *my* vote—"

Bettina's frown shut her up her instantly. "Sally! You know the rules. Our votes are anonymous, remember?"

Sally nodded so vigorously that Linus lost his hold on her nipple. The two-year-old's frantic wails had her shifting him to her other breast.

"And last but not least, there is also Kelly Bryant Overton, and her little boy, Wills," Bettina announced. "The Bryant name is 'old San Francisco,' if you get my drift."

Drift? The committee was practically gagging on the inference. "Old San Francisco" meant that Bettina—whose own lineage went back to the Gold Rush on this side of the country and to New Amsterdam on the other—had probably grown up with this Kelly person. If that were the case, did Bettina expect two of the six votes to go to her personal connections?

Or was there only one vote they'd have to give up? Was her relationship with Lorna Connaught in name only?

She'd said it herself: already they had more boys to choose from than they needed. There was one knock against the Connaught tot, as well as the Overton kid. In any regard, the other moms and tots—that Jade person and her son, Oliver and all their dot-com connections; the cute twin girls with the well-connected father; Ally, the ballet patroness-slash-lawyer's wife and her sweet little girl, Zoe; the eco-friendly professor's wife—

It was all so damn confusing!

For the first time in the club's history, every member of the committee came to the same conclusion, at the same time:

They would vote for whomever they wanted, Bettina be damned.

Everyone sat silently until Bettina, obviously still annoyed, muttered, "It's time to take a vote."

Since its inception six years ago, the club enjoyed the enviable dilemma of too many candidates for so few spaces. Always one to let power go to her head, Bettina, who relished her founder status, took it upon herself to establish an intricate voting system that would resolve any annoying ties.

Not that there should be any. As far as she was concerned, Bettina had clearly expressed her own desires.

She led everyone out into the hallway where she handed each of them four safety pins. "We'll walk back in, one by one, and drop a safety pin in the piggy bank of the candidates we feel are worthy of an open slot. Kimberley, you'll go first."

Solemnly, the women nodded. Kimberley got up and walked back into the room, voted, and returned.

Mallory did the same. Then Sally. Then Joanna.

Bettina went last. When she was done, she called them back in. "Time to count!"

It only took a minute.

Each piggy bank contained the same number of safety pins: four.

Stalemate.

Bettina shook her head in amazement. "Ah. Well. Seems like we're going to have to go again. This time, we'll reverse the order. So let's all rethink any weak links."

A second vote would break any stalemate.

In theory, yes. In practice, not so much.

Those who live in the picturesque and well-heeled neighborhood of San Francisco's Pacific Heights have, on occasion, enjoyed an excursion or two to France's renowned capital city. Having done so would have exposed them to the torrid history of that country's revolution, which culminated with the severing of the head from the body of its regal, albeit tyrannical, king. Perhaps it was that spirit the members of the Pacific Heights Moms & Tots Club application committee channeled when, once again, they voted their consciences.

And again.

And yet again.

Liberté, égalité, fraternité. Democracy is a stubborn trait.

Even Sally couldn't be cowed. In fact, she had the audacity to mouth the unspeakable: "So, why not just let them all in?"

Bettina shook her head emphatically. "No way! PHM&T playgroups have always been equally populated. This is why when someone drops out, we do an open call and vet the candidates the same way. And besides, it would make this year's Onesies larger than any other playgroup, which sets a very bad precedent. It tells people we can't make up our minds."

What she wasn't saying—but they all knew—was that the key to the club's success was its exclusivity. Ten toddlers per preschool year only. No excuses. No ifs, ands, or buts.

"I'd like to make a suggestion," The way Mallory's eyes glowed left the others to wonder if chants and curses were involved. "Why not have the six applicants compete for the four slots? They'll prove they deserve it by earning it."

"Brilliant!" Bettina exclaimed. "Just like that *Survivor* show, but the prize is so much greater."

Taken aback at the compliment, Mallory blushed. It was the first time any of the others had seen her face flushed with anything other than anger.

"We'll call it a probationary period," Bettina continued, warming up. "The applicants will be judged on their social connections, their personal grace under pressure while hosting an event, and of course, their toddlers' sociability. Then, at the end of the first sixty days, we'll vote someone off. At the end of the next sixty days, another applicant bites the dust. The last four standing are the victors. And once again, we've got a perfect Onesies Group." She clapped her hands with delight. "I'll get out the invitations first thing tomorrow."

CHAPTER THREE

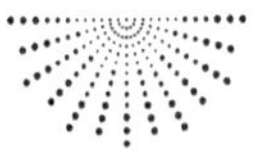

Wednesday, 5 September

CONGRATULATIONS!
You are now a member of the Pacific Heights Moms &
Tots Club!*
Your Inaugural Play Date takes place on Monday,
September 10, 10am at
The James Leary Flood Mansion, 2222 Broadway, in
Pacific Heights (of course!)
RSVP Bettina Connaught Cross at
TopMom4Ever@phmtc.com

*Pending the successful completion of your probationary
period. Details to follow.

CHAPTER FOUR

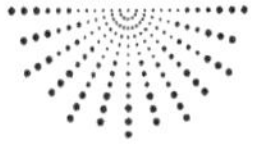

Friday, 7 September

"—GOT IT! IT ARRIVED YESTERDAY IN THE MAIL." THE STIFF wind took Clarisse Tanner's nonchalant words and carelessly tossed them over her shoulder at her jogging partner, Jillian Frederick.

Every day, come rain or shine, Jillian laced up her sneakers and jogged out of her house on Pacific Street and around the corner to Baker Street, then down to Lombard and beyond Chestnut Street in the Marina district and on to Crissy Field with her one-year-old twin daughters, Amelia and Addison, in tow. On Tuesdays, Thursdays, and Saturdays, Clarisse joined her, strolling her two-year-old son, Travis.

Invariably, by the time they reached the midpoint of their jog—Fort Point, under the Golden Gate Bridge—

Clarisse was huffing and puffing. "I don't know how you do this seven days a week," she groaned. "Three days a week is more than enough torture!"

Jillian's grimace gave Clarisse the false impression that she agreed with her. In fact, Jillian loved running.

It was the best way to run away from her fears.

By now her life should have been perfect. She had quit college in order to work as a waitress in order to support Scott, her husband, as he finished his undergraduate and master's degrees in finance. After he'd finally gotten a job as an associate in one of the largest financial management firms in San Francisco, her role in their marriage took on one she enjoyed: moving them from their tiny studio in the basement of an ancient Victorian walk-up in San Francisco's North Beach, to a roomy (albeit even shabbier) townhouse she'd found for them on one of the most desirable streets in Pacific Heights. With its view of San Francisco Bay, and the fact that it backed up to the wooded and wondrous Presidio National Park, the house was a dream come true. Granted, its rock bottom price reflected its condition. The townhouse needed a new everything: foundation, wiring, and plumbing.

"I can't take on a project like this," Scott had warned her. "I'm working twelve hour days, and I'd rather be golfing on the weekends."

"I hear you loud and clear. I promise, come weekends, we'll both be on the links. And just think, from here, we're mere minutes from the Presidio golf course." She wrapped her arms around his waist and smiled up at him.

"The asking price is much less than we bargained for. I'll use the balance for the renovations and supervise the work myself. I can do that, now that I'm not working. And on the weekends, we'll both work on our handicaps."

Reluctantly, he agreed.

Long, exhausting days were the norm for both of them. The house's transformation became a five-year labor of love for her. She turned it into a showcase with elegant moldings, arched doorways, and large picture windows that allowed its breathtaking views to be admired from every room.

As for golfing, on most weekends, while she managed whatever workmen and handymen were lurking about, Scott made it out to the course without her.

In time, Jillian gave up golf altogether and took up jogging. It was less time-consuming, and the positive effects on her body were much more gratifying.

When Scott finally made partner in the firm, he was just as reluctant when she told him about her next project —having a baby.

"A kid? Aw, hon, I don't know." His smile was wary, tired. "When will I ever see the little bugger?"

She was so surprised at that question she laughed out loud. "When you get home, silly! And you'll have weekends, too, to play with our child. You'll just have to give up golf." It was a joke, of course.

Apparently he didn't think so. "But I like golf."

"Good. You can teach it to your son." Her determined smile never wavered.

In anticipation, he bought a full set of toddler-sized U.S. Golf Kids golf clubs, which he placed in the nursery beside the window.

That she was carrying twins wasn't as disappointing to him as the fact that both the babies were girls. "I guess this means our shot at a boy goes out the window." He sighed.

"Next go-round, right?" She meant that in all sincerity.

"What, are you crazy? Two is more than enough. Besides, there are no guarantees it'll be a boy."

She never had the nerve to ask him why he'd taken the toddler clubs out of the nursery and what he had done with them.

If she thought he'd give up his weekend rounds of golf after the girls were born, she was sorely mistaken. While he golfed, she jogged with the girls in tow. Rolling their Bugaboo Donkey Duo stroller up Divisadero gave her biceps other women admired, not to mention an ass that turned men's heads.

But the only man whose head she ever wanted to turn was Scott's.

Unfortunately, these days he was too busy to notice.

Jillian had no doubt that Clarisse had timed her dire announcement about the Pacific Heights Moms & Tots Club to take place here at the base of Fort Point so they'd at least be near a bench, should Jillian want to sit and talk about it.

Appropriately enough, it was also a convenient place for jumpers who wanted to end it all.

Jillian wasn't that upset, but yes, talking it out might keep the tears at bay until she got the twins home in time for lunch and their baths. "How do you know the invitations went out already?"

"A big-mouthed birdie told me. I ran into Sally Dunder, the Twosies' group mom, inside Whole Foods. She says it was such a close call that they're trying something different this year, whatever that means. It will be announced at next Monday's meet-up, when the Onesies group is introduced to the rest of us." She tightened little Travis's hat. Already, she'd lost his pacifier to the brisk winds. "Bottom line: those who got in should have received their invitations by yesterday. Of course, the brunt of the applicants were long shots anyway."

"What does that mean?"

"Between you and me, they look down their noses at working moms as well as single moms. And while no one will just come out and say it, I'm guessing they're not too fond of anyone who isn't at least a size four, either."

"I'm married, and I'm a stay at home mom. And I'm in shape—"

"'In shape?' Sweetie, with all the jogging you do, I'd say you're more like a *minus* two! My guess is you have a hard time keeping the weight *on*."

Jillian shrugged. Yes, she was overdoing it. But she liked being lean.

And Scott liked her slim.

These days, though, she couldn't tell if he liked her at all.

She couldn't think about that now. The last person she'd ever tell there was trouble in paradise was Clarisse, who knew everyone's business.

That's why she's the perfect person to ask why I wasn't chosen for PHM&T's Onsies group, Jillian thought. "What do you think they had against me?"

"Got me." Clarisse sighed. "Scott is well-placed. But they try for an even number of boys and girls. Maybe the fact that you have twins blew your chances."

Jillian shook her head angrily. "Well, I'm not going to leave one on someone else's doorstep just to get into the darn club! I guess I could have faked having just one daughter and brought a different one to every other play date—you know, like *The Parent Trap.*"

Clarisse snorted at the thought, but the pitying look in her eyes was all Jillian needed to know that her friend felt sorry for her.

"Got to go! Someone's coming by this afternoon to give a bid on refinishing the deck." It was a lie, but Jillian couldn't stand sitting there any longer. She jumped up from the bench and stretched, then trotted off, stroller in hand.

She could hear Clarisse panting to catch up, but she refused to slow down for her.

Clarisse certainly wasn't waiting for her either, so why bother?

11:33 a.m.

Jillian couldn't remember a time Scott had been home mid-morning on a Friday since he'd started at Colby & Trask, not even when he was sick with a cold.

In truth, he was barely home at all anymore.

He must have heard the front door open, not to mention the click of the stroller's wheels as she rolled it over the granite floor of the entry foyer, and yet he didn't bother turning around.

Instead, he stared out the big picture window, at the bay out beyond the Palace of Fine Arts.

The run up the hill was like a sleeping tonic for Addison and Amelia, so she left them in the stroller but whispered, "Honey, what's wrong? You don't have a fever, do you? The girls couldn't have given you something, because neither is sniffling—"

When he turned around, she realized it had been too long since she'd truly looked at his face. The grooves in his forehead were deeper than she'd ever remembered. The hair beside his temples was completely gray.

And his eyes were red and damp. He sighed heavily. "I want a divorce."

If she hadn't still been holding onto the stroller, she would have collapsed to the floor.

"What? Why?" She looked down at the girls in a useless attempt to collect her thoughts. All she could think about was how she should take them out of their tiny jackets before they got too overheated, and then go through the motion of preparing their lunch—

Anything but listen to Scott explain why he wanted to destroy the life they'd built together.

"I'm sorry, Jillian. But the truth is that I'm in love with someone else." He refused to look her in the eye, but he guessed her next question. "It's Victoria."

His assistant.

Ah, now it all made sense.

It was always Victoria who stayed late with him at the office. And it was Victoria whose calls he took at all hours of the evening, with the excuse that "the China deal has a few details that we've yet to pin down..." or "It's a conference call with Singapore. The investor has questions on the prospectus."

Lies, lies, lies.

"She's pregnant, Jillian."

"Pregnant?" Jillian couldn't believe her ears. She had to ask, "Boy, or girl?"

"It's—a boy. Not that it matters."

"You're lying."

He flinched but didn't deny it. Instead, he rubbed salt in her wound, the worst way possible. "I love her, Jillian. It wouldn't be fair to either of you if I stayed with you."

"*Fair?* Don't talk to me about fair! I gave up college and waited tables for you!"

So he couldn't see her cry, Jillian looked down into the stroller. Amelia was fussing in her sleep. Jillian knew she should pick her up, peel her out of her coat, and stroke her back to calm her down—

But no. She'd wait until after he left. Then she'd grab both girls and run with them up the staircase.

He didn't deserve to see them ever again.

He didn't deserve them at all.

Not that he'd care. Now that he was getting the boy he'd always wanted, he wouldn't ever make time to see them anyway.

But he'd make time for his son.

Just like he had made time for Victoria.

"Enjoy the view. It's the last time you'll see it. I'm keeping the house."

"Yeah, I figured as much. And with what you'll be getting as alimony once the lawyers get involved, I guess I'll be paying for it, too."

"You better believe it. Not to mention the property taxes. That's what I call 'fair.'" She was proud that she was able to keep her voice steady.

As he walked passed her, he murmured in her ear, "Then I guess we both got what we wanted."

No! she wanted to scream. I wanted you. I wanted us. I wanted this.

And all these years, I thought you wanted it too.

Her slap left him reeling. It echoed off the two-story-high ceiling, waking both the babies.

Scott hesitated just a moment, as if fighting the instinct to reach in and pick up his daughters. Because they happened so rarely, the memories Jillian treasured most were those of him holding both of them in his arms, cooing down at them, his head rocking back and forth as he peered into each of their little faces.

You can't stop caring for them, she pleaded silently. *Even if you don't love me anymore, you can't stop loving them, too.*

When he didn't pick them up, she took them instead: one on each hip, rocking them to keep them from reaching out to him.

Their happy squeals for their Dada were hard enough to take.

Obviously, he couldn't take it either, because he headed for the door. "The mail is on the table. I took mine. I'll have the rest forwarded to the office."

He nodded toward the tortoiseshell bombe beneath the large ornate mirror that graced the foyer wall below the winding staircase. She'd found both pieces at an estate sale for a pittance and refinished them herself.

Maybe I should have been working on my marriage instead, she thought.

The door creaked when he closed it. Jillian stood there staring at it for at least five minutes. All that time she fought back the tsunami of tears that made her head want to burst. The girls' responses to her silence were to babble back at her. To yank her ponytail. To hug her around the neck.

To giggle and reach down, toward the floor.

They're right, she thought. *We have to keeping moving forward, with or without Scott.*

She forced herself to do something normal. What were Scott's last words? Oh yes, something about mail…

That's when she saw it, right on top of the sales flyers and the Restoration Hardware catalog and the latest issue of *Elle Décor*:

The invitation for the Pacific Heights Moms & Tots Club.

She and the girls had been accepted into the club.

They'd be able to meet new people, make friends, network, get on with their lives—

As long as the club didn't find out about her pending divorce.

If and when that happened, they'd be considered an inconvenience.

"They won't find out," she said out loud. "We deserve to belong. I've worked too hard for it."

No matter what, the club would be her daughters' entrée to everything she'd hoped for.

She wanted to believe that so, so badly.

CHAPTER FIVE

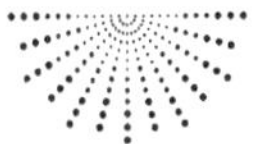

Monday, 10 September
8:36 a.m.

"You're not seriously taking Dante to Bettina's shindig dressed in that tuxedo, are you?" The shocked look on Matthews's face said it all: overkill.

Since receiving the Pacific Heights Moms & Tots Club invitation, Lorna had been floating on a cloud. For three days she had scoured the town's baby boutiques for the perfect outfit in which he'd make his club debut. When she came across the tiny tuxedo, she had actually squealed out loud, scaring the poor shop girl out of her skin.

Stunned by Matt's remark, she shook her head. "But… he looks so adorable in it, and it's Armani—"

He was laughing so hard he choked on his coffee.

"Hon, he's not meeting the Pope! It's just a bunch of babies drooling all over each other."

Matt's belly laugh normally made Lorna feel as if everything was right with the world. Today, though, all it did was reinforce the fact that nothing was as it should be.

But Matt's reaction had her wondering if Bettina's would be the same. She could just imagine her sister-in-law's tight lips curling into a smirk.

Yep, nix the baby tuxedo.

She sighed. It had taken her almost fifteen minutes to knot Dante's tiny bowtie, what with him squirming the whole time. She had learned fast that he didn't like her touching him around his neck. With his long dark tendrils and those big blue eyes, he'd be the handsomest child there. But in life, looks only took you so far. The other mothers would be comparing him to their children, scrutinizing everything about him. His height and weight. His agility. His laugh, and the other noises he made. It was hard to admit that anything about Dante seemed out of place, but yes, his disinterest in walking and talking—his naturally quiet demeanor—did concern her.

He's got plenty of time to catch up, she reasoned. *No one is perfect, but he comes darn close.*

As for today, his appearance would be his calling card. All they had to do was get through the morning, and they wouldn't have to worry about fitting in for the next four years of his life. Longer even, considering the friendships they'd be making.

She nodded grudgingly at Matt. "Okay, maybe a tux is a bit overboard. Since you want to play Tim Gunn on *Project Runway,* make yourself useful, and help me decide what he should wear. We've got to be fast, though. Dante and I have to be at the inaugural meet-up in less than an hour."

She picked up Dante, then grabbed Matt's hand and led him into the nursery. Everything that had been hanging in Dante's closet lay on the toddler bed beside his crib.

"My second choice is this." She held up a navy long-sleeved cowl sweater with miniature chino pants. "It's Ralph Lauren. Understated, wouldn't you say?"

"Nah. He'll look like he just came back from the country club in that get-up."

Lorna's eyes widened. She wanted the other moms and tots to envy them, not despise them. "Good point." She reached for her Plan C: a monogrammed sweater vest over a pale blue Oxford shirt with khaki shorts.

"Do you have anything without a polo player or monogram?" Matt asked as he pulled open one of Dante's bureau drawers. "Jeez, Lorna! Even his T-shirts are designer. What did you do, buy out the store?"

Lorna crossed her arms over her chest. "Our son deserves the very best."

"He's not in prep school. Hell, he's not even near *pre-school.* Shouldn't he dress like a toddler?" He shut the drawer, opened another and rummaged around. "This is more like it." He pulled out a miniature red, white, and blue tracksuit adorned with the London Olympics logo. "This has 'stud' written all over it, don't you think?"

"And why, pray tell, would I want the others to think of him as 'a stud'?"

Matt grabbed hold of her arm and pulled her down onto the bed with him. "Girls like studs. You wouldn't want them to think he's a mama's boy, would you?"

The prickly little hairs from Matt's perennial five o'clock shadow never failed to arouse her. Lorna didn't mind at all—except this morning. This morning was devoted to Dante's launch into polite society.

Reluctantly, she pushed him off and stood up. "What's wrong with that? I married a mama's boy, and I wouldn't have it any other way."

Matt's smile disappeared. "Thanks, Lorn. Just what I need to hear."

"What? You know I didn't mean it like *that.* All I was trying to say is—"

He rolled off the bed and walked out the door, slamming it behind him.

Damn me, why did I say that?

Matt's sensitivity to Eleanor's role in his life as his chief form of income—at least until one of his hair-brained online schemes hit it big—had always been a sore spot. Okay, yeah, it irritated her that he was able to slide through life on his family name—not to mention their largesse—unlike Lorna, who had come from nothing and had worked hard to make good enough grades to get accepted to U.C. Berkeley on scholarship...a scholarship that bore the Connaught name.

Matt had been the one who awarded it to her. Then he asked her out.

Of course she turned him down.

She held strong through three months of insistent phone calls, but the six straight days of two-dozen yellow roses sent to her room at Berkeley's Cloyne Co-op finally convinced her to give in. She got tired of her roommates teasing her that her dorm smelled like a flower shop.

"What do you care? The rest of this place smells like a men's locker room," was always her reply.

Still, she couldn't help but be flattered by his attentions.

It wasn't until a year later, when he'd asked her to marry him, that he confessed it was love at first sight.

"Why is that?" she had asked. This was, after all, Matthew Harrison Connaught.

"Because I knew you'd love me despite my name. Why else would you have played so hard to get? I haven't worked this hard for anything in my whole life."

His answer had been such a surprise that she laughed out loud. To cover up her embarrassment, she retorted, "I think you work harder at your fantasy basketball picks. Still, I'm flattered, and I'll try my best to have made it worth your while."

"No need. Now that you're mine, my life is complete. We can both relax." His declaration came with a kiss.

He'd been wrong about her motives. Of course she

loved him. But if she was honest with herself, his name had been the prime attraction. It inspired awe in others, like from those in the university's fawning fundraising staff. It also elicited the envy of her friends. Most importantly, being seen on Matthew Connaught's arm opened many doors she'd always longed to enter, but had only been allowed to peek through.

Before him, she was nobody. Now, she belonged.

Granted, without his name he would have been just another good-looking San Francisco slacker. Cute, yes. Fun to flirt with, hang out with, and to ruminate about world hunger and politics, without a doubt...

But would she have married him?

Lorna didn't know. But she did know she longed to run after him now; to beg his forgiveness, even though they both knew she hadn't said it to hurt him.

Watching from the window as her husband stalked out of the house and down the street, it struck her once again how truly different they were. Unlike him, she could never sit back and let the Connaught name carry her. She had too much pride.

She was grateful that as a Connaught, Dante would always enjoy financial security. But she was determined for him to make his own way in the real world. Dante's successes would have to come from him and him alone.

With her help, of course.

In fact, if she'd had her way, Dante would have used her surname as opposed to Matt's. That way, unlike his father, he'd never allow himself to be burdened by it, or use it as a crutch. Best yet, no one would presume his many future accomplishments came from his family name and connections. He would take pride in being a self-made man.

But she knew better than to suggest this drastic move to Matt. It would crush him, and she loved him too much to hurt him that way.

Instead, she would work that much harder to make Dante just one of the guys.

For starters, that meant looking like one. The cute little tracksuit would do just fine.

9:44 a.m.

"A divorce is never easy, Mrs. Frederick. But you do have a lot working in your favor. Especially the fact that he's left you for another woman only a year after you gave birth to two infants, and you've been a stay-at-home mother because of that." Tom Lutz, Jillian's divorce lawyer, nodded toward Addison and Amelia, who were half-toddling, half-crawling on the very expensive Persian rug that graced his hardwood floors.

This initial meeting with Lutz had already run a full twenty minutes over the allotted hour, and the girls were getting antsy. Jillian could have kicked herself for not expressing her breast milk the night before so she could have brought it with her, but she hadn't counted on being here this long. The girls' first Pacific Heights Moms & Tots Club was starting in less than ten minutes. Considering

Lutz's office was all the way downtown, even if she hustled the girls out in the next ten minutes or so, by the time she got their stroller to the car and drove to the meeting, they'd still be twenty minutes late.

So much for a good first impression.

She scooped up Amelia, buckling her into the stroller's back seat. By the time she'd turned around, Addison had crawled under Lutz's desk. Instead of picking her up, though, he scooted his wheeled chair away, as if she were carrying the plague or something equally undesirable. Addison giggled, crawling even faster to catch up with him.

Realizing he was cornered, he had no choice except to grab her.

Addison promptly spit up on him.

What didn't end up on the lapel of his $3,000 wool-and-silk Brioni suit landed on the rug.

The terror in Lutz's eyes was not lost on Jillian. She had no doubt he'd be adding the dry-cleaning charges to her bill.

She swapped him a dry cloth diaper for her daughter. "Mr. Lutz, thanks for all you're doing on our behalf. As for our home, it's only fair that I hold on to it, isn't it? I may not work out of the house now, but I was our sole source of income while Scott was in school. And I found the house and renovated it. He—he couldn't care less about it."

Lutz's lids closed as he considered her question. Or maybe he was reconsidering her as a client. She still remembered his pained grimace when she bumped the girls' stroller against his antique side table.

"As we discussed, Mrs. Frederick, California is a no-fault divorce state, which means the court will consider an equitable division of assets acquired after the marriage. Keep in mind, though: 'equitable' doesn't always mean 'equal'. And considering the underlying circumstances, he may be open to signing over his portion of the house to you. But be expecting some quid pro quo."

"What do you mean by that?"

"For example, you're asking for full custody. He may take issue with that."

"I doubt that." Jillian blushed when she heard the quiver in her own voice. She busied herself by shaking one of Amelia's tiny dolls in front of her daughter's face, so she wouldn't have to look at Lutz.

The last thing she wanted was for him to see the tears welling in her eyes.

"Even if Mr. Frederick gives you the deed to the house, there is the question of the mortgage payments, not to mention annual property taxes. If he doesn't cover those as well, you'll soon find it a hollow victory."

He had raised his voice, not to make his point, but because both girls were making it known that they were hungry and cranky.

Aw, heck, Jillian thought. I can't just whip out both of my boobs and feed them now. If I did, Lutz would be the one throwing up.

Scott had also averted his eyes whenever she nursed

the girls in front of him.

That son of a bitch…

Jillian forced her lips into a smile before turning back to face Lutz. "Yes, he should be making the house payments and paying all the taxes. Isn't that what alimony is for?"

Lutz nodded. "So, you'd rather go for alimony than child support?"

Jillian shook her head, confused. "What's the difference?"

"Child support provides you with a stipend for the girls' expenses until they reach the age of legal majority, which is twenty-one." He was now trying to talk around the twins, who were crying. "Alimony is paid directly to you. You could do with it as you wish, with certain stipulations. For example, should you remarry, he would no longer have to provide spousal support."

"Ha! The way I feel now, I never want a man to touch me again."

Lutz shrugged. "If I had a dollar every time I heard a client say that, I'd be a very rich man."

By the looks of it, he was well off without collecting on that bet, considering his retainer was $600 per hour. Jillian frowned. "Aren't we eligible for both?"

It was Lutz's turn to smile. To smirk, actually. "We can ask for anything. It doesn't mean we'll get it. That is what the judge will decide. "

"What about the prenup I had signed? It was stupid, really. Scott suggested it, in the hope that his parents wouldn't cut off their support while he was in college. They insisted that he was 'marrying beneath him.' Even after I signed, they cut him off anyway, so a lot of good that did."

"I'll look it over. Some of its clauses may be struck down, but it depends. For the most part, the good of the children is the first consideration. However, depending on how it's written, issues such as his infidelity may not be of any help to us."

Jillian felt like she'd been kicked in the gut. Having gotten Victoria pregnant was an even bigger wrong than had they been merely fuck buddies.

He looked at his watch. "We'll be filing the papers for the legal separation later today. My assistant, Tara, will ring you the moment the petition for divorce is ready for your signature. Then we'll serve Mr. Frederick. At his office, I'm guessing."

Good, Jillian thought. *That should embarrass the hell out of both him and Victoria.*

"Tara will also be handing you a checklist of things you'll need to do as soon as possible, like closing all joint bank accounts, making a list of all assets, pulling the paperwork on savings and retirement accounts, those sorts of things. If he's got an employment contract, you need to get a copy of it." Lutz stuck out his hand to shake but pulled it back. Instead, he hesitantly patted her back. "My assistant also has your invoice on her desk. You can make the necessary arrangements regarding payment with her."

Time to pay the piper, Jillian thought. "But I didn't bring a checkbook."

He was practically shoving her and the stroller out the door. "That's okay. We take credit cards."

Tara waited until Lutz closed the door before handing Jillian his bill. Jillian's eyes bulged. "Forty-eight hundred dollars? But I was only in there for two hours! I thought it was six-hundred dollars each—"

"We bill the first eight hours in advance," Tara explained sweetly.

Jillian fumbled in her purse until she found her Visa card and handed it over.

Tara swiped it, then frowned. "Oh dear! Declined. I guess Mr. Frederick has already had it cancelled."

"What? Can he do that?"

Tara's nod was sympathetic. "We see it all the time. If I were you, I'd head down to the bank. He may have closed your accounts there as well."

I can't do that now! Jillian thought. I've got to get the girls to the meet-up! Oh hell, this is a nightmare.

A tear dropped from her cheek onto the assistant's desk. Patting Jillian's hand, Tara murmured, "Don't worry. I'll bill you for it. But hit the bank as soon as you can."

Jillian was too choked up to do anything but nod.

She practically ran down the hall to the elevator. By now the girls were so hungry they were wailing.

She waited until the elevator started its descent before she allowed herself to cry, too.

9:52 a.m.

"Well, well, well! Aren't we the early birds!" Bettina's tone was all sweetness and light as she reached out for Dante. Once he was in her arms, she dismissed Lorna with a wave of her free hand.

Lorna had already made up her mind that nothing Bettina did today would get under her skin. But then Bettina stared down at Dante. "What is that, a tracksuit? Omigod! You've dressed him like some little old Florida retiree!"

Lorna's retort—that it was Ralph Lauren; that it was official Olympic gear; that Matt had chosen it for him—stuck in her throat as the room filled with more moms and tots.

Most of the other little boys were wearing tuxedos.

If not a tux, then monogrammed sweaters and khakis.

Had Matthew been standing beside her at that moment, Lorna probably would have kicked him. Hard. Then she would have ordered him to run home and get Dante's tuxedo.

Instead, she stood there like a lump while Bettina introduced "Dante Connaught, and his mother, Lorna," to two other women who gushed reverent thanks for the honor of being there.

In fact, one of the women—Chakra Crutch—proudly said, "I made Quest's tuxedo myself—out of hemp! My husband, Stone, and I *eschew* synthetics. Plastics, too, for that matter. In fact, we live our lives entirely green."

Who the hell actually uses the word 'eschew,' Lorna thought as Bettina and the other woman, Kelly Overton, cooed admirably over the little boy's duds. Then Kelly did a double take and turned to Lorna. "Oh, so you're a Connaught? Then you must be married to Bettina's brother, Matthew." Kelly shifted her son, Wills, onto her other hip and held out a hand to Lorna.

"You know my husband?" Lorna asked as she shook it.

"Ha! You bet I know Matty! Why, Bettina and I practically grew up together. She'd be the first to tell you I had a crush on her older brother. He's still adorable, I presume?"

Lorna didn't like the way Kelly had practically purred his name. Her only consolation was that Bettina was just as annoyed. No one else would have picked up on Bettina's ire, but Lorna had been around her long enough to know that whenever she smoothed her hair behind her right ear, she was pissed about something.

She waited until the women drifted off to the buffet table before asking Bettina, "It sounds like she knows Matt pretty well. Why is that?"

Bettina shrugged. "We all prepped together at Lick-Wilmerding."

That's when it hit Lorna. "Bettina, if that Kelly person hadn't caught my last name, no one here would have known we were related."

"That's the point." Finally, Bettina was smiling again.

"I'd rather that it not become an issue—I mean, should you ever have to leave the club."

"What does that mean, 'should I ever have to leave'? The invitation said—"

"The invitation specifically mentioned a probationary period. Seriously, Lorna, with your lack of attention to detail, I'm surprised you actually graduated from Berkeley." Bettina's giggle was accompanied by a shrug. "To be perfectly honest with you, this year we're in a bit of a pickle. Too many great families for too few slots. There's still some weeding out to do. So let's all pray you don't somehow screw up Dante's chances here at PHM&T, because we both know I don't, and can't, play favorites."

Ha, Lorna thought. What you mean is that you won't play favorites with me, but you certainly will for your BFF, Kelly.

Lorna waited until her voice was steady. "I would never presume that you would," she said.

"So glad we're both on the same page. You deserve to pat yourself on the back, Lorna. For once, you got somewhere all on your own." Bettina didn't excuse herself. She just handed Dante back to Lorna then walked toward the women and children who were now flowing through the doorway.

Lorna had a good mind to grab Bettina by her fake blond roots and pummel her into the ground. To stomp that smirk right off her face. To yank off one of her suede Prada platform booties and beat her to death with it.

But no, of course she couldn't do that. It would set a bad example for Dante and the other children.

Besides, there were too many witnesses.

And as much as she'd like to, she couldn't run away, either. She had to stick it out, for Dante's sake.

She sighed deeply and tickled him under the chin in the hope that he might smile. When he didn't, she reasoned that her perceptive little man felt her pain.

He probably knew his Aunt Bettina was the cause of it, too.

From now on, whenever she read him a fairy tale, she knew what name she'd substitute for the word "witch." It started with a 'B'. And no, it wasn't bitch.

As her heart swelled with love for her son, she smiled and hugged him even closer. "Come on, Stud, let's go impress all these cute little girls."

10:15 a.m.

Knowing the Pacific Heights Moms & Tots Club's Official Onesies Inaugural Play Date had been underway for the past fifteen minutes was driving Ally Thornton crazy. Flocks of mothers with children rushed through the gated entrance of the Flood Mansion and up its grand old stone staircase, but all Ally could do was watch from the backseat of her BMW X6 SUV while Ellis Conway, the chief executive of the online shoe company, Foot Fetish, droned on and on about the finer points of the latest inventory procedures.

To make matters worse, Ally was missing half of what he was saying because Zoe, her fifteen-month-old daughter, kept tossing her Baby Stella dolls into the front seat. Each time Ally retrieved one, Zoe would squeal, then send yet another doll over the headrest.

"Okay, Zoe, game over," Ally whispered. Her cell phone was on MUTE, but she hoped that leading by example would silence Zoe.

As if *that* would ever happen.

"No! Babas! *BABAS!*" Zoe shouted as she motioned toward the front seat, where her dolls had flopped, like drunken sailors after a beer binge.

"*Shhhh!*" Ally warned her daughter. So that Zoe could be buckled into her car seat, Ally handed her a sippy cup.

Not a smart move. Zoe slapped it out of her mother's hand. The top popped off, and Ally's chest was hit with a wave of milk.

"Bad girl! Bad, *bad* girl!" she hissed as she scrounged in Zoe's diaper bag for a cloth to wipe herself off.

If she thought it would shame her daughter into silence, she was sadly mistaken. Instead, Zoe screamed gleefully as she climbed out of her car seat.

Ally had just grabbed hold of one of Zoe's plump little legs when she heard Ellis say through her cell phone's earbud "For its approval, I presented to the board a list of proposed options to be granted to company employees and its advisors. Ms. Thornton had previously mentioned a concern regarding the initial stock split. Ally, would you care to elaborate?"

Ally quickly tapped her cell phone's MUTE OFF button so her corporate board members could hear her.

Big mistake. At that very second Zoe let loose with a banshee cry. Then, with her tiny fist, she grabbed the cell phone and tossed it out the window.

"Ally! Are you there? Are you all right?" The last voice Ally heard before the moving truck ran over it was that of Barry Simon, her corporate attorney.

Well, thank God he had attended the meeting on her behalf. He'd make something up so the board wouldn't think she'd been eaten by an anaconda or something.

Barry had been her best friend since high school. He was also Zoe's sperm donor, and in Ally's will, he shared the responsibility of Zoe's legal guardianship with his lover, Christian Cordell.

Not that the Pacific Heights Moms & Tots Club would ever know that. On her application, Ally and Barry had presented themselves as a happily married couple.

Nor would the club find out that Ally Thornton hadn't *completely* stepped out of the workforce to care for Zoe: she was still working part-time as the chief strategy officer of Foot Fetish. Her reconnaissance of PHM&T had warned her that the application committee frowned upon working moms. By putting down "board member in an advisory capacity," she sidestepped the issue of how much time she was obligated to spend at the company.

Ally had mentioned that she had been accepted to the club only the day before, during Barry and Christian's weekly Sunday dinner together with her and Zoe. Barry had laughed so hard he'd spewed his martini. "Ally, my sweet, tell me you're kidding!"

Ally, who had been mixing the salad, put down the tongs with a thud. "And why is that funny? All anyone on the playground talks about is how PHM&T is *the* club to join."

Barry winced as the last drops from the martini shaker trickled into his glass. "I don't know about that. One of the biggest jokes around Christian's hair salon is all the hoops that club makes its members jump through. If you think the Bracknell lackeys are giving you grief with their macho corporate games, just wait until you meet that woman—Christian, what's her name again?"

"*Bettina* Connaught Cross." Christian shook his head gravely. "All my customers gossip about her. They say her name is apropos: you '*cannot* cross' her, or you're out of the club. Their horror stories could curl your hair."

"Which is why you do so many Keratease treatments."

Barry's joke earned him a raised brow from Christian.

"We all know that's the last thing I need." Ally shook her head. Her long, dark curls, which spiraled down her back, bounced from side to side. "Seriously you guys, how bad can it be?"

"Oh, it would be okay," Christian had chimed in, "if you were a brain-dead stay-at-home MomBot who angsts over whether you gave up breastfeeding too early because you pulled the poor kid off your tit before she started grade school. But that's not you, Ally. And you know it."

Barry's brow shot up. "Well, well, well! Someone is being a bit too catty."

Christian shrugged. "Nope, sorry. You can't accuse me of that. Hell, if it had been up to Ramona, I'd still be suckling."

Barry laughed. "You're right. You're such a mama's boy."

They were only kidding, but that didn't stop the tears from welling in Ally's eyes. She'd always felt guilty for never breastfeeding Zoe. But how could she? Bracknell International's offer to buy Foot Fetish had been proffered in the fifth month of her pregnancy. The deal had closed the day Zoe was born. Her dream—to sell the company, so she'd have enough money to raise Zoe without ever having to work again—to put her through college, without the fear of her daughter incurring debt to get her degree, like she had—had finally come true.

With one caveat: Bracknell International insisted she stay on as the company's chief strategy officer for at least three years.

The offer had been too tempting to refuse, especially after BI had accepted Simon's counter: besides taking home a seven-figure salary and additional stock options, she'd only have to show up at the office two days a week in order to participate in design sessions, vendor relations strategies, and the monthly board meetings.

For those days, she had lined up a great nanny: Lucy Sweetin, a grandmother to three strapping grown boys, all San Francisco firefighters.

A corporate board hadn't been easy to get used to. Before Ally had sold the company, she'd had only one person to answer to: herself. Her style was to make snap decisions. Now she had bean counters who questioned her every move.

The worst of them was the CEO, Ellis.

But she also had the financial freedom that any mother would envy.

And she'd done it without a man at her side.

Working all those long, late nights was easy when you were going home to an empty house.

Her twenties had been a decade of missed opportunities and heartbreak. The decision to have Zoe meant that at least she would enter her forties with someone at her side. Someone to grow with and with whom she'd share experiences.

Someone who would always love her.

Now that she and Zoe had been accepted to PHM&T, the good times were about to get even better.

Ally had smiled up at Christian. "You know better than to listen to gossip. I'll finally have an opportunity to bond with other moms while Zoe socializes and plays. It's a dream come true."

Barry frowned even as he kissed her forehead. "Be careful what you wish for, Al."

Now, even as she patted down the wet stains on her blouse and stared out at plastic shards and crushed circuit board that used to be her cellphone, Ally Thornton knew that her sweet Barry had nothing to worry about.

She grabbed her bag, scooped up Zoe, and ran through the mansion's front gates, right behind some tall man with a baby boy on his shoulders.

10: 24 a.m.

The man may have been over six feet tall, but this didn't seem to bother his toddler son, who sat high on his shoulders and chortled as he yanked at his father's thick, blond hair.

Mallory, who along with Joanna had been handing the guests their name tags, saw him first. She nudged Kimberley, who had been handing rose corsages to the new Onesies moms: red for legacies, and white for those six moms who would be competing for the four other slots. She grimaced at his audacity and signaled Bettina with a wave.

If anyone was going to tell this guy that this was a private party, it had to be Bettina. Kimberley was much too shy to the point of blushing as deep red as her hair, Mallory would be rude about it, and Joanna was too big a flirt to tell him to get lost.

Bettina sighed as she straightened her shoulders. By the time she'd reached the intruder, her lips were pursed into a benign smile.

10: 25 a.m.

"Wow, Oliver, look at all the cute babes that are here."

Brady Pierce's murmur was low enough that he may have truly been addressing his son, but certainly loud enough for the stately blonde with the SnoCone simper to hear it, too.

It was for her benefit, anyway.

As Brady had expected, it didn't exactly stop her in her tracks, but the pale pink flush rising from her neck to those high cheekbones was proof it had the desired effect.

For a second, at least. Then the icy smile was back. "I'm sorry, but this is a private party."

"The Pacific Heights Moms & Tots Club, right?" Steadying his son with one hand, Brady reached inside his jacket pocket with the other and pulled out the official PHM&T invitation. "I'm Brady Pierce. My son, Oliver, made the cut."

By now he was used to the effect his name had on others. The cloud of wariness that had darkened her cornflower blue eyes now brightened in anticipation of how she could use this new relationship to her advantage.

Brady was not above letting her take advantage of him —if it got him what he wanted, too.

Bettina honored him with a dimpled smile. "Oh! But… well, we assumed he would be here with his *mother*. It's Jade, isn't it?"

"This is Jade's charity morning. She sits on Save the Children's Celebrity Council." He shrugged modestly, as if on his wife's behalf. "But this is so important to her—to *us*—that I promised I'd stand in for her."

He was lying. Wherever Jade was—and his security

team had yet to figure that out—more than likely she was sleeping off a hard night of clubbing.

Not to mention that Jade hadn't seen Oliver in months.

No matter. Had Jade shown up, this ice queen, and all these other buttoned-up mommies, would have been appalled at the way she'd try to navigate the mansion's stone steps in her too short, too tight skirt and thigh high boots. He could just imagine them rolling their eyes whenever her oversized breasts jiggled under whatever clingy, low-cut top she'd chosen to wear that day.

Not to mention the gasps they'd give when one nipple just happened to pop out.

If that happened, she couldn't even use the excuse that she was still nursing Oliver.

Brady wondered if he were nuts to presume these sorority types would arrange play dates with a platinum blond bombshell who thought the Kardashians were high society. He might have been stupid enough to fall for a big-titted pole dancer with a face like an angel, but none of them would.

Unless he was successful in winning them over first. Otherwise he couldn't accomplish his end game: to get Oliver into the group.

At least he had Madame Ovary on his side. She had winked slyly at him when he entered and then pretended to be surprised to see him there.

SnoCone was there for him, too. That was obvious by the way she patted his arm gently and purred, "I'm the club's founder, Bettina Connaught Cross."

"Nice to meet you." He drilled her with his best "I'm all yours" gaze for a full ten seconds before scanning the room. "And which of these little angels is yours?"

Bettina sighed mightily. "Unfortunately Lily—she's in the Foursies group—had to miss this year's Onesies inauguration. She still has four more weeks of ballet camp, in St. Petersburg."

"Isn't Florida a long way for a four-year-old to go by herself?" Brady asked.

"Florida? Heavens, no! The *real* St. Petersburg, in Russia. She's practicing with the grand masters at the Kirov."

Brady's eyes grew big. "But…isn't she a little young for that?"

Bettina nodded nonchalantly. "My daughter's talents are unparalleled. But nature thrives on nurture. Besides, it's never too late to train for the Youth America Grand Prix." She pointed to the buffet. "Enough about my little prodigy. Feel free to stop by the refreshment table, and introduce yourself and your little genius to the other members. If you'll excuse me, now that everyone seems to be here I'm going to introduce you, and the other new Onesies group, to the rest of the club. Mallory at the front desk has Jade's corsage. I'm sure she'd be delighted to pin it on you instead. Please tell Jade that we look forward to meeting her at the next meet-up on Wednesday. Her devotion to our little group—and yours—is truly appreciated."

Booyah! Brady thought. We're in.

Unless Jade screws it up somehow.

10:31 a.m.

"You know you're leaking, right?" Chakra Crutch's tone said it all: *Loser.*

Ally had pinned her corsage over the largest of the milk stains on her sundress, the one over her right nipple, which was the size and shape of a volleyball.

Unfortunately, the corsage wasn't large enough to cover the other stains, too.

It was on the tip of her tongue to tell the woman that it wasn't a leak at all, but a spill. She bit her tongue. That would surely earn her a lecture about the harm she'd done Zoe in choosing not to breastfeed.

Nope, she didn't need that now, especially from a woman whose name was a New Age catchphrase. (Chakra? Oh, come on! *Really?*) Ally was already self-conscious about how she was dressed for the occasion. Her sundress was a casual cotton print, and she had put Zoe in a romper since this was supposed to be a simple meet-and-greet for the new one-year-olds and their parents. So why all the Armani, Gucci, and Ralph Lauren?

And that was just the toddlers. Their moms were decked out in Pucci, Cavalli, and Michael Kors.

Not to mention all those boys in their miniature tuxedoes, like Chakra's little Quest.

Granted, the mansion's opulence encouraged such formality. Forget paper plates and plastic spoons. Real silverware and china adorned the buffet table, which was a regular groaning board of delectable finger foods and decadent sweets.

Like the piece of red velvet cupcake she handed Zoe before popping the rest of it in her mouth.

Noting how the little girl squealed, Chakra glared at her, appalled. "Those things are obesity time bombs! With so much fat and sugar in their diets, half the children in this room will have diabetes before they reach their sixteenth birthdays! Not to mention all that red dye is toxic! And you're nursing, too!" She shook her head in horror.

It also leaves a permanent stain, Ally thought. I guess she'll hit the roof when she finds out Zoe had wiped the back of Quest's hemp tux with red icing.

The woman needed to chillax, big time.

Ally took little solace in the realization that she wasn't the woman's only target for criticism. Chakra had started off by complaining about the reception room ("It's certainly not child-proof! All it takes is one two-year-old to slip on these marble floors, and you've got a kid who's a vegetable for the rest of his life...") before turning a sharp eye on the other mothers. "I find it appalling that those women over there," she pointed toward the quintet of Twosies mothers who stood by the French Doors leading out to the mansion's gardens, "won't allow their children to sleep in the same bed with them. Why wouldn't they? It was good enough for our ancestors, it should be fine for us, too! Modern Western society sells its soul for the privilege of sleeping on a feather top Serta. No wonder our children grow up hating us."

Ally shrugged. "Maybe they'd prefer not to have their kids in the room while they make love."

"Sex?" The woman's smile curdled into a grimace. "Who has time for sex after children?"

Ally was the wrong person to answer that. The break-up three years ago with her last boyfriend had planted the seed for her journey to single parenting. She'd been ready to commit herself to a full-time relationship, whereas he wasn't. If not a man, then why not the child she'd always wanted?

While she never regretted her decision, sometimes she wondered if, between work and tending to Zoe, she'd ever have sex again.

"How about you and your husband—Barry, isn't it? Do you co-sleep?"

Chakra's question had taken Ally completely off guard. "Barry and me? Heavens, no, we don't sleep together! I mean, *with Zoe*."

"Oh." That one word reeked of Chakra's disdain. Finally, she picked up a mushroom cap, sniffed it, and put it back. "Processed. Figures." She fingered the broad strap of Ally's sundress. "The way you're leaking, I'd stay away from these mushrooms—*and* these synthetic fabrics. Just another reason to go organic."

Ally pursed her lips to keep from responding with something she'd regret later.

Apparently another mother standing nearby was

thinking the same thing because she rolled her eyes and whispered, "Don't mind her. I nursed up until a month ago. You wouldn't believe how many shirts I ruined. But hey, anything to keep them healthy, right?"

The woman nodded toward the cute little boy she was holding. He looked to be around Zoe's age and size, and was dressed in an adorable little tracksuit with the Olympic crest.

No tuxedo, thank goodness, Ally thought. Well, at least one of these moms is normal. "I'm Ally Thornton. And this is my daughter, Zoe. She'll be fifteen months on Thursday."

"Pleased to meet you. I'm Lorna Connaught. And this is Dante." The woman turned slightly, so Ally could get a better look at her son. But just then he turned his head again, so what she faced instead was his head of dark curls.

"A handsome little guy, isn't he?" Ally gently stroked the back of his head. "Did you say Connaught, as in the club's founder?"

Lorna shrugged. "Yes, but don't hold that against me."

Ally was so surprised by that comment she laughed out loud. But before she could ask what Lorna had meant, Bettina Connaught Cross tapped a fork to her crystal water goblet three times. All the chatter ceased.

"Ladies…and gentleman, if I may have your attention! I'd like to introduce our new Onesies group—both its legacy moms," Bettina paused and took a deep breath for emphasis, "and those who are currently contingent members, whose mettle will be tested with all the new and wonderful challenges they'll face this year."

Those wearing white corsages—Ally, Brady, Chakra, and Kelly—opened their eyes wide in confusion.

Only Lorna's smile stayed benign. In no way did it betray what she was thinking:

Hit me with your best shot.

10: 53 a.m.

Thank goodness the mansion's entryway had a ramp, which allowed Jillian to wheel Amelia and Addison's stroller right into the reception hall. Carrying both girls from the only parking spot she'd found, some eight blocks down the street, would have been horrendous, and it would have made her later than she already was.

The very pregnant woman who handed over her name tag put her finger to her lips. "You're just in time. Bettina is making the introductions now." As Jillian pinned on her corsage, the woman eyed the stroller longingly. "Lucky you! A Bugaboo DonkeyDuo! Talk about the Mercedes of strollers."

Jillian nodded. "I've been very pleased with it. Especially with these two." She nodded down at the girls who were sleeping despite the ruckus of gossiping moms and chattering toddlers and preschoolers. Having expended all their energy in tearing up Tom Lutz's office, they were finally worn out.

The woman patted her belly. "Mine will be boys. But

they'll have to make do with the one I bought for their older sisters. Four kids means a lot of hand-me-downs and sharing. That's a great thing, I guess."

She pointed to two girls—one four, one five—who were holding hands in front of the buffet table, staring up longingly at the cupcake tower.

Jillian nodded empathetically. Things were about to get tight in the Frederick household, too.

She followed the woman into the reception hall and immediately recognized the speaker, having seen her pictures so many times in the *Nob Hill Gazette*: Bettina Connaught Cross.

"One of the joys I have as founder, is the opportunity to introduce the very few—the 'chosen,' as I call them—into our little family." Bettina's gaze swept through the room. "When I call out your names, please wave and tell us just one fun little *bon mot* about yourself. I'll start with our legacies!"

There were six families whose Onesies already had siblings in the club: Bella Adams with her son, Liam; Hillary Trumbull and her daughter, Ava; Marcia Broderick and her daughter, Ella; Janine Ledbetter and her son, Jackson; Doreen Landau and her son, Ethan; and Gwen Markham and her son, Nathan. Each woman blushed with pride as she tried to sum up, in a sentence or two, something about herself that she hoped would make her seem nice or kind or interesting to the others.

Everyone wants to fit in, Jillian thought. Just like me.

She had wandered closer to two moms who also wore

white rose corsages. Ironically, the only man in the room was standing next to them. He, too, wore a white rose.

The final legacy to speak, Marcia, tossed her long, dark mane before giving a nonchalant shrug. "Ella is already showing a prodigious sense of style. She helped me pick out this ensemble!" She twirled around so the other moms could oooh and ahhhh at the pairing of her 10 Bar striped jacket and white Philip Lim slim trousers with a Helmut Lang sheer top and Miu Miu platform pumps.

"Ah! Barney's," Lorna murmured.

"As in, the purple dinosaur?" Brady said it just loud enough for Jillian, Ally, and Lorna to hear. When Ally tried to hide her laugh in a cough, Lorna slapped her on the back.

The commotion was not lost on Bettina, who honed in on the four of them. And her frosty tone was not lost on them. "I see our newbies are excited about meeting all of us. Lorna, why don't we start with you?"

"Me?" She paused. "Yes! Well, I'm Lorna Connaught… and…" Her voice faltered from embarrassment. She hadn't expected to be the center of attention so soon, and had been listening closely to the other mothers' introductions. She refused to sound as needy as Bella, or as desperate as Hillary, and certainly not as smug as Marcia. But now that Bettina had all eyes focused on her, the words she'd so carefully chosen flew out of her head. "… and this is my son, Dante. I think he's perfect, so I guess I'm not much different from anyone else here."

"Except for the fact that you're related to Bettina,"

Mallory muttered.

Yes, everyone in the room heard her. The memories of their own hard-fought entries into PHM&T were probably what weighted down their previously airy smiles into knowing frowns.

In the white-hot glare of their stares, Lorna's cheeks flared from pink to red. But before she could retort, Bettina purred, "One couldn't ask for a sweeter sister-in-law. Rest assured, as was the case with each and every one of you, Lorna's eventual inclusion here will be secured only by her meritorious deeds on the club's behalf."

Confusion darkened the eyes of those sporting white corsages. *Eventual inclusion? What the hell did that mean?*

Lorna couldn't believe her ears. Favoritism? She might as well hang a placard around my neck that said, 'Pariah! Don't talk to this woman, or I'll snub you, too!'

"Which brings me to a change implemented this year by the Pacific Heights Moms & Tots Club application committee." She paused. "It's no secret that every year we are inundated with applications. While reading through them, we keep the club's mission in mind: to choose families who we feel are worthy of our children's precious time." She let the words sink in before continuing. "But considering there are only ten family slots each year, it is quite an endeavor to choose families we know will honor that mission. This year we have six legacy families." Bettina honored them with a half bow. "Your previous efforts on behalf of the club are why your places have already been secured. However, we also have six new families who will be competing—that's right, I said *competing*—for the four final slots."

She paused for the inevitable gasp that echoed through the room and the dismayed looks from those wearing white corsages.

"What we'll be asking from you isn't anything you wouldn't want to do anyway for us, your new, dear friends. Of course, attendance is key. So is your participation in our special events, such as our Halloween parade, our after-Thanksgiving potluck and recipe cookbook, our holiday parties, our mom-and-tot field trips, and our parent's-nights-out. Sounds like fun, doesn't it?"

She waited for the awed nods, as the new members realized that the club wasn't just a social diversion, but a way of life.

"Then, there are our charity fundraisers—like today's! Don't be shy about adding your name and donation amount as soon as possible, so others can applaud you." She pointed to the large white board on the far side of the room. "Today's donations benefit the pediatric clinic at Pacific's Dugoni School of Dentistry. In fact, each and every one of you will be assigned hosting duties at these wonderful events. Trust me, it will be fun as well as challenging."

Her smile promised the world on a platter—after days of grueling work.

"Unfortunately, two months from now—November 2nd, to be exact—then two months later, after New Year's Day, a probationer will get word that they lacked the necessary…oh, how shall I put it? Verve? Drive? *Savoir faire*? The women in this room are proof that you'll need all of that and more to join *our* ranks."

Our ranks. Upon hearing that, those wearing white corsages wilted in unison.

"Four families will certainly have something to celebrate! But, sadly, there are six families to choose from." She sighed at their dilemma. "I'll leave you with this classic quote: 'May the odds be always in your favor.'" She raised her arms, as if embracing the white corsages. "Now, on with our introductions…"

11:08 a.m.

That is so like Bettina, Lorna thought. Pitting parents against each other, as if it were some elaborate social experiment! She knows what it means to each of us to be here. And now we've got to go through the indignation of some sort of parenting death match? I should walk out, right now…

And let Bettina accomplish her goal of chasing me away?

No. Never, Lorna swore to herself. Bettina is right about one thing: Dante and I are here on our own merits. For whatever reason, the committee wants us here—even if Bettina doesn't. Apparently, Bettina's opinion isn't the only one that counts.

Maybe Barry is right, Ally thought. Why do I have to prove myself to these women when I've already proven myself to Wall Street?

She looked down at her daughter, who was laughing and giggling and playing on the floor with Jillian Fredrick's twin girls.

But I'm doing this for her, she thought. No, really I'm doing it for us. I've run a company with two thousand employees. I've wooed investors, and I hold my own with a boardroom filled with sharks waiting to cut my throat. How hard can it be to impress these women? It'll be a cakewalk. A run in my pantyhose. A bad hair day.

Hopefully, one that won't last five years…

Fuck. Oh, fuck, Brady thought. Why didn't Madame Ovary warn me about this bullshit competition?

Prepping Jade for it would be damn near impossible. Of course, his security team would have to find her first. Until then, he'd have to buy some time—or better yet, he'd buy them off.

He walked up to the charity whiteboard. With a flourish, he wrote his name along with Jade's, and the amount of five thousand dollars. Altogether, the donations already posted didn't equal his alone.

He waited until the awed gasps and applause died down. Then, in the humblest tone he could muster, he said, "If Jade was here, I'm sure she would insist we double that. I know I speak for both of us when I say thanks for including her and our little Oliver in this wonderful community."

His wink, directed at Bettina, took her by surprise. Self-consciously, she smiled, then unconsciously, she pushed her hair behind her right ear.

Madame Ovary also saw this. Only she wasn't smiling.

OH MY GOD, JILLIAN THOUGHT. WE'RE SUPPOSED TO LEAVE A donation? I have no money! But I've got to fake it, for the girls' sake.

She made her way to the white board but hesitated before writing in a figure. After Brady's grand gesture, anything else would seem puny. Whatever happened to the saying, "It's the thought that counts"?

She only had a twenty on her. Her credit card surly wouldn't work, and she was afraid to write a check in case it bounced.

Still, she wrote down $100. She'd scrounge it up somehow.

"He's making us all look bad, isn't he?"

Jillian turned around when she heard the voice of the pregnant mom with the two preschool daughters. She tried to smile back at her, but all she could do was nod.

And pray she could sneak out the back with Amelia and Addison before someone cornered her for her donation check.

A sudden thought came to her. She hesitated before saying it out loud. "Listen, if you want, I'll sell you my stroller. For half price of course, since it's used. It's practically brand new, though."

"Wow! Really? For only six hundred?" The woman's eyes opened wide. "But why would you do that?"

"My mother-in-law just gave us another stroller, and I don't want to insult her. You know how it is. But I certainly don't need two. So, are you interested?"

"Sold!" The woman opened her purse. "Thank goodness I went to the bank this morning." She counted out twelve 50 dollar bills. "Will this do?"

"Yes, of course." It was a little less than half the retail value of the stroller, but what else could Jillian do? She needed money badly.

She made sure to smile as she handed Bettina two of the bills.

A friend watched the woman's children so she could walk Jillian to her car and help her shift the twins, their dolls, blankets, and the phonebook-sized PHM&T Membership Manual, from the stroller to the backseat.

Jillian drove away, toward the bank, to see if Scott had cleaned out their account. If so, the five hundred dollars would have to last at least until the end of the month, minus the cost of any reasonably cheap double stroller she could find on Craigslist as soon as possible.

In the worst-case scenario, she'd be eating baby food out of jars along with the girls. But they would survive.

CHAPTER SIX

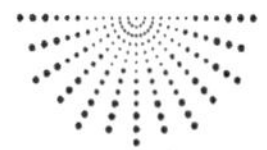

Tuesday, 11 September

JADE PIERCE'S EX, BRADY, WAS CUDDLING THEIR SON, Oliver, by the large picture window when her airport limo rolled to a stop in front of his home. Jade could feel Brady's eyes following her as she rose from the Lincoln Town Car and sauntered up the curved walkway toward the front door.

For just this moment she had practiced walking in the tortoiseshell patent leather Manolo Blahnik pumps until her stride was fluid. The shoes had not been her first choice, but to her surprise, the personal dresser at Bergdorf-Goodman had nixed the pair she'd chosen: sparkly Giuseppe Zanotti multi-strapped sandals with four and a half-inch heels.

"It's too...well, let me put it this way—that shoe is a favorite with the ladies of the night," the woman said.

Figures, Jade had thought to herself.

To drive home the point, the personal shopper pointed to the Chanel jacket she'd hung in Jade's dressing room. "The sheer blouse you love goes perfectly with this jacket. Sexy and elegant, but not skintight."

Jade had almost crowed at the woman's attempt at subtlety.

Ha! I guess all it takes to go from whore couture to 'sexy and elegant" is a few hundred dollars, she thought.

That definition also worked for the pencil-straight skirt, which hugged her high, firm ass: the pay-off from eight-hour shifts, five days a week, at the Condor Club.

That, and a chance to meet big spenders like Brady Pierce.

Heck, she'd wear a nun's habit if it would win Brady back.

Her one and only goal was to be the Jade he had wanted all along.

If she could make him believe this, they'd both get what they wanted.

HE STILL LOVES ME. JADE REVELED IN THIS REALIZATION.

This she knew, despite his hesitation to grasp the hand she held out to him.

In spite of the guarded look in his eyes.

What gave him away was the way in which he hugged her: so tightly, as if he were afraid to let her go. As if he were vowing to himself, *Never again…*

Jade's heart pounded hard against her chest at the blessed realization that the person she loved most in the world might have finally forgiven her. That he would want her to stay there with him, now and forever:

Oliver.

If only Brady felt the same way, she thought sadly.

At least she'd always have her son's love …

Or would she? It might take years, but the obvious joy the little boy was now showing—the way in which he bounced and squealed in her arms—could dissipate over time, in the hot bright reality of maturity. How long would it take before the infant's idolatry of his mother gave way to the child's scrutiny of her emotional flaws? By the time he was a teen, would he detest her?

Brady would make sure that he did.

Unless he was willing to forgive her, too.

The smile she gave Brady was filled with the confidence that someday he would.

If only he'd smile back.

JESUS, SHE'S EVEN MORE PATHETIC THAN I REMEMBER, BRADY thought. Look how she clings to Oliver, as if he's a life raft. At least she's toned down the hooker hair. And the clothes aren't so bad...

Man, she's got a great ass.

That thought would have gone straight from his head to his dick, bypassing his heart entirely, if at that very moment she hadn't smiled up at him.

But she did. Not only that, but her lower lip was quivering, and her eyes were glazed with tears.

So that he wouldn't feel sorry for her—so that he wouldn't want to take her in his arms and kiss her and strip her down and make love to her, and tell her he forgave her—he forced himself to remember that the only reason she'd come was because there was more money in it for her.

In other words, she was the most expensive piece of ass he'd never have again.

If he thought that would make him go soft, he was wrong. It only made him want her more.

"I'M HERE BECAUSE OF *SOME MOMMY CLUB*?" JADE COULDN'T believe what she was hearing. All this time she thought he'd finally forgiven her.

That he missed her.

Oh hell, she could see he missed her. Why else was he rock hard?

But he hadn't come near her. He'd kept his distance, and his eyes were stony. Even his smile seemed carved in granite.

"Yeah. Simple as pie," he answered with a shrug.

"Here's the deal: I'm quadrupling your annulment payoff for the next five years."

"What?" Jade's eyes opened wide.

Brady nodded. "You heard me. For half a mil a year, you'll take Oliver to his playgroup three mornings a week. You know, yack it up with the other moms there. In fact, make friends with these ladies. They're a nice enough bunch." He hoped he sounded convincing enough. Well, at least Lorna, Jillian, and Ally seemed normal. It would be a shame for them to be eliminated, but what the hell. Last man standing.

And that man would be Oliver—*if* Jade could do her part and pull this off.

"It'll be fun, you'll see. Sometimes the group goes on field trips. You'll enjoy that, right? And you'll be asked to host a get-together or two. Oh, and they have these big-ass holiday shindigs. You'll be asked to help out at those. Whatever they want, just say 'yes.' Otherwise you'll get Oliver kicked out of the club, and the deal's off. And the big thing—any kid he likes, you can invite over here."

"'Over here'? You mean you want me to move in?"

The hope in her voice made him wince. "Not exactly. The in-law-suite downstairs will be yours. It's got its own kitchen and media room. And a separate entrance—"

"So, you're hiring me to be my own son's nanny?" Jade pursed her lips. "That's sick, Brady. Even for you."

"Sick? Hell, Jade, I thought you'd jump at the chance to be a part of your son's life! But I guess it's easier to take the money and stay away—"

"No! That's not what I meant… it's just that…well, if I'm going to truly be a part of his life, I need to be up here. With him. With both of you."

"No. That's not happening." He shook his head adamantly. "Look, I'm just asking for three hours a day, three days a week. It ain't brain surgery."

"That's not parenting."

"You're right, it isn't. And since you're not ready to be a parent, I guess it's a perfect solution, wouldn't you say?"

Jade's eyes grew dark with anger. "Who says I'm not ready?"

"Seriously, you want to go there? You always were a glutton for punishment. Okay, for starters, you ate junk food during your pregnancy, even though I *repeatedly* asked you to stop—"

"That nutritionist you tethered to me was a Nazi! It wasn't as if a few Doritos and Coca-Colas could hurt the kid! I mean, come on, already, Brady—"

"Then, after Oliver was born, you never even considered nursing—"

"But that's because…well, I…I thought you *liked* how my breasts looked," she said, looking down at them now.

"I do… I mean, I did! Quit interrupting me. I'm trying to make a point here." He closed his eyes as he shook his head. Nope, the vision of her breasts was still in his mind's eye.

Stay on point… Stay on point…

"Jade, half the time you were with him, Oliver had

diaper rash—because you were afraid of breaking an acrylic nail when you changed him! You rarely held him—"

"I was always afraid I'd drop him." She blushed at how silly the truth sounded.

He shook his head in disbelief. "Not to mention you preferred to be out partying with those girlfriends of yours than to stay home with him."

"I did stupid things, I know it now." Jade sniffed away one tear, but another rolled onto the tip of her nose anyway. "It's just that after the pregnancy, I wanted to feel like me again."

Brady shrugged. "Jade, I get it, you were twenty-one when you got pregnant with Oliver, and obviously you weren't ready for motherhood. But Oliver can't afford your mistakes. That last one almost cost him his life! Leaving our son while he had a fever, no less—with that creepy so-called talent manager of yours, so you could audition for some damn porn film? Our son almost died because that idiot didn't know enough to call me, let alone take him to the emergency room. If I hadn't come home early…" The memory of that day rolled over Brady. He had to shake his head to block it out. "Fuck it, Jade! What were you thinking?"

The tears trickling down her cheeks were sooty with mascara. She did nothing to wipe them away.

"I thought—I thought you didn't love me anymore, that's what I thought! I thought you had regretted marrying me in the first place, because you were a somebody, and I was a nobody. I thought my body was no longer pretty to you." She swallowed hard in order to choke down the emotions that, until now, had stayed inside. "I thought that, if I did something special, if I got the role and it made me just as famous as you, that you'd —*that you'd love me again.*"

Love her.

But that that's just it—*he had never loved her.*

Lusted after her, absolutely. What man wouldn't?

Not that he could say that to her. He didn't know what to say. Sure, he could string her along so she did what he asked. Hell, that would certainly save him a load of dough...

But, no. Not this time. In the end, he'd be breaking her heart.

He couldn't do that again.

He took a deep breath. "Listen, Jade. Right now the most important thing in my life is Oliver. I stopped working and sold my company to be with him. Do you know why? Because I want him to have the one thing my father couldn't give me: time. And unlike me, I want him to finish college—a really great one, like Stanford or MIT or Harvard. But first, he has to get into some really good schools. And for that he'll need all the right connections—which was something I never had. Hey, we're already lucky; he has your looks, and my brains and money. But we both know the world is an ugly, cruel place, and he'll need more than that. Good schools will motivate him to do something with the gifts he's already been given, to make something of himself and not just piss it all away."

Did she get it? He couldn't tell because she just stood there, not saying anything.

Finally, she nodded.

"Good. Then we're both on the same page." He exhaled. "This is strictly a business arrangement."

"You don't get it, do you Brady? I don't want your money. I want you. And if I can't be part of your life, too, then I can live without being in Oliver's. Because it will always be a package deal."

She was right.

But if he let her back into his life, he'd never have the life he truly wanted.

He remembered the sense of calm that had come over him when, finally, Jade was out of his life. Oliver was to be his sole focus. But he had also envisioned finding a partner. She'd be gorgeous, sure, but she'd also be smart and funny.

Best of all, she'd be strong enough that she'd never question his love for her.

And his money wouldn't matter.

That person could never be Jade. As much as he'd once hoped that could be the case, he'd found out the hard way that it wasn't.

And Oliver had almost paid the ultimate price for her thoughtlessness.

Jade was always filled with doubts. Jade never acted; she reacted, and her instincts were wrong. Always.

"I'm out of here." She brushed Oliver's curls with her lips, then practically tossed him to Brady so she could grab her bag and head for the door.

What the fuck? No, he couldn't let her go.

With Oliver in tow, he started after her.

She was almost through the foyer before he was close enough to grab her arm. He yanked her to his side. They stood there, face to face, staring at each other over Oliver's head—

Until he kissed her.

The more she resisted, the harder he got.

He hadn't understood how desperate Jade was to be a part of his life, too—

Until she put her hand on his dick.

At her touch, he almost exploded.

BRADY HELD TIGHT TO OLIVER AS JADE UNDID HIS BELT. Then, she took him in hand. Her fingers caressed him slowly at first, but soon they clenched him tighter, pumped him quicker. With each stroke he groaned and rocked their son in his arms. Oliver gurgled, as if it were all some game.

He was right about that.

And she'd won when Brady slumped into her arms.

Within the tight cocoon of their group hug, Jade felt the rapid thumping of Brady's heart. Oliver's was beating even faster.

But hers had to be pounding the loudest. Her love for Oliver knew no bounds. But neither did her love for Brady. She'd called his bluff, and it had paid off.

She'd been doing that to men all her life.

She would not be sleeping in the in-law suite.

CHAPTER SEVEN

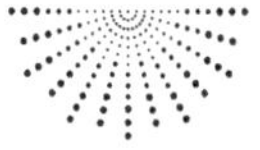

Friday, 14 September
7:48 a.m.

SHE WAS DREAMING ABOUT SCOTT AGAIN.

It was practically the same dream that always haunted Jillian right before she woke up: they were both still in college, and he'd skipped class one morning so they could linger in bed after sex. Back then their lovemaking was furtive, as if every second were precious. Really it was, since his classes were on an earlier schedule than her waitressing shifts.

In the dream, Scott's kisses had just given way to penetration with his very large thumb and forefinger. Jillian could feel herself getting wetter, and he seemed to grow large in her hand. She whispered in his ear that he should come inside her *NOW! OH PLEASE NOW.* He nodded and heaved himself over her. He was huge and hard when he entered her. So huge that she moaned in pain—

In joy.

And then her cell phone buzzed.

She was so shocked to hear it, she fell out of bed with a thump.

"Mama up up! Mama up up!" The twins squealed in unison.

As she sat there on the floor, her eyes moved upward toward the bed—no Scott, of course.

Just that damn buzzing phone on the nightstand.

"Who is it?" She wondered if the shame she felt emanated through the ethersphere that enveloped all 21st Century technology.

"The judicial hearing takes place this morning, at eleven o'clock." It was Jillian's attorney, Lutz. "Sorry for such short notice, but they rang my assistant at five yesterday to say they had an opening. Considering your financial status, she was sure you'd want us to take it."

"Yes! Of course." Lutz's prediction in that very first meeting had been right. Before Jillian could stop him, Scott had wiped out all of their joint checking and savings accounts and had cancelled all the credit cards.

With each unanswered call by her soon-to-be ex husband, Jillian had gotten more anxious.

Well, now it was time to see what the courts could do about it.

"Glad you're game, Jillian. Now, to make our point

that you need money as soon as possible, I'd suggest you show up with your kids."

She pulled the cell phone away from her ear, as if staring at it might make Lutz, and the divorce, and Victoria, all go away…

And Scott would come back to her. Wishful thinking.

Her lust for Scott dissipated in the sun's bright glare emanating through the bedroom window. "But—but I can't today! We've got our mom-and-tots group meeting—"

"You're kidding me, right? You'd ruin your chance at child support and alimony, for a play date? *Lady, this is your children's future!*"

He was right.

Bettina would just have to understand.

But no, Bettina would not understand. Bettina would make her leave the club.

"I—I get it. I'll be there." She hung up, then went to her bookshelf and found the PHM&T manual she'd received at the inaugural meet-up and turned to the page marked EMERGENCIES, where Bettina's phone number was listed. Her hand was trembling as she punched the numbers into her cell.

"Yes?" Bettina's voice was curt.

"Hi, Bettina, it's Jillian Frederick, in the Onesies. I am so sorry, but Addison, Amelia, and I won't be at meet-up today—"

"Oh?"

That one word syllable was all it took for Jillian to lose her cool. "Yes! Well…you see, we—the girls are…*sick!*"

"Oh." Bettina's silence seemed to go on forever. "Well then, I commend you for keeping them home. The manual clearly states that the sick and infirm are not, under any circumstances, to attend. The last thing the club would want is a pandemic on its hands."

Jillian nodded vigorously at the phone. "Yep, for sure."

"Is what they have infectious?"

Bettina's question caught her off-guard. "What? Oh, yes! But I'm sure they'll be tip-top by Monday's meet-up."

"Good. In the interim, scrub them vigorously."

With a click, Jillian was off the hook.

11:06 a.m.

"What is *she* doing here?" Jillian hissed at her attorney, then nodded toward Scott's definitely pregnant assistant, Victoria.

Lutz shrugged. "Moral support."

"Moral what?" Jillian's voice was so loud, he had to shush her. "You mean *'immoral support'*, don't you?"

"Call it what you will. He's trying to make a point."

"Yeah, I get it. The point is that he knocked her up, and he'd rather be with her." Jillian shifted her head away from the twins, so they wouldn't see her cry.

Amelia and Addison had spotted Scott, too, because they squealed, "Da da! *Dadadadadada!*"

Instinctively, he waved at them, but seeing Jillian's glower, he turned his head in shame.

Good, Jillian thought. Stay away from us. And keep her away, too…

As if reading her mind, Scott smirked, stood up, and walked over.

But when he tried to pick up Addison, Jillian slapped his hand away. "Don't even think about it." Her voice trembled, but he shrank away at the threat.

"All rise," the bailiff shouted.

Jillian looked up to see the judge had witnessed it all.

Including the girls crying for their father.

She sank into her chair, praying.

1:08 p.m.

It's over, Jillian thought. For good. Just like that.

She'd been with Scott since their second year in college. She'd dropped out in her senior year in order to support him when his family had abandoned him.

They'd been a team through thin and thin. Team Scott and Jillian.

No, it now hit her: *it had only been Team Scott.*

Throughout the proceedings, his eyes went from the judge, or to Victoria.

Never to Jillian.

At the best time possible—for *him*—he had glanced longingly at the children: that time being when his attorney had asked for joint custody.

The twins hadn't made it easy for Jillian to make her case for sole custody. Despite holding them both in her lap, they had squirmed and cried. At one point, Amelia had shouted, "Dada!" More of a command than a question.

At Jillian's behest, Lutz had pointed out, "Your honor, Mr. Frederick works long hours, and practically seven days a week. The point is not to leave the children with a nanny, but to ensure they have their mother."

"What will happen when their mother goes to work?" Scott's lawyer countered.

I wouldn't have to, if Scott did the right thing, Jillian thought.

I wouldn't have to, if we weren't going through this hell…

The judge wavered—too long, in Jillian's opinion— before shaking her head and mandating an every-other-weekend edict instead.

Then, with a clack of a gavel, it was over:

Life as Jillian knew it. The life she thought they both wanted.

Now she knew better.

Afterward, Lutz explained to her that Scott's request for joint custody was a typical ploy. "He figures the more he sees of them, the less he'll have to pay out."

Jillian shook her head in anger—at herself, mostly. "I guess it worked. The judge gave him every other weekend! Not only that, but she mandated he pay me only four thousand dollars a month—despite the fact he makes almost half a million dollars a year! That's a pittance for him, but it's only the equivalent of the mortgage note on the house. That means I'll have to come up with the rest: for the utilities, food, clothing, and property taxes. Not to mention childcare, since it's obvious I'll have to start working again."

Lutz shrugged. "It's a temporary mandate. And don't forget, she ordered him to turn over half of everything that was in your checking and savings accounts."

"There wasn't much there. Only a few hundred."

"I'm guessing he was planning this for a while and stashed the brunt of his savings in a few accounts you know nothing about."

As pragmatic as Scott was, she guessed Lutz was right.

Still, there was a part of her that hoped he'd come to his senses. It had to be obvious to him how much the girls were missing him. Maybe he truly missed them, too.

Maybe she'd been too hasty to slap his hand away.

She had been stupid to let him walk away without a fight.

This whole thing is one big misunderstanding that has snowballed out of control, Jillian reasoned. Perhaps if we met and talked things through—

I can convince him to change his mind.

And he'll come home.

Now that she'd calmed down, she could control her anger. She could openly discuss with him whatever it was that drove him away and into Victoria's clinging arms.

Even if it meant going to the whore's apartment to do so.

She found the address online: a Russian Hill high-rise co-op.

7:22 p.m.

Since she couldn't afford a babysitter, she had begged Clarisse to take them that night. "This thing at Scott's firm came up at the last minute, and I can't find a babysitter to save my life. If you take them tonight, I'll take Travis for you twice. Deal?"

Clarisse gave her a funny look. "I heard you missed your Onesies meet-up because the girls are sick. If that's the case, I don't think I should expose Travis to whatever they have."

"No need to worry. In fact, the doctor gave them a clean bill of health just this morning."

Jillian held her breath as Clarisse processed her response.

"Well...I guess it can't hurt. Okay, I've got them covered. You two have fun."

Fun.

Yessirree, ringing all the security buzzers in the whore's building until one of her neighbors let her in was a blast.

As was slipping into the elevator and up to the pent-house floor, where Victoria lived. With Scott.

And knocking politely was certainly worth a chuckle.

"What do you want?" Victoria's wary voice carried through the door.

That was expected, since Jillian was standing directly in front of the peephole. "I have to speak to my husband."

Silence. Forever, silence.

"Scott, I know you're in there!" Jillian hadn't meant to raise her voice, but she couldn't stop herself. "I saw your car parked down the street."

"Jillian, just…just go away." Scott's voice hit her like a wall of contempt.

Go away? Just like that?

She smacked the door with her fist. "Of course I'm not going away! We need to talk about what's really going on here, Scott."

"Jillian, this is why we have attorneys, to take care of the tiny little details. Now, go home."

Go home?

Fuck you.

"I'm not just some detail you can pawn off on a lawyer! I'm your wife! I gave you thirteen years of my life! I bore your children! And you expect me to roll over and play dead just because you ran off with your pregnant whore?"

Scott stuck his head out the door. "Don't call her that!"

Down the corridor, two other doors opened to see what the ruckus was about.

Step right up, folks, for tickets to the show, Jillian thought.

"I can call her anything I want, *she's sleeping with my husband, the father of my children—*"

"You see? That's just my point, Jillian—"

"What's your point? That I made a beautiful home for you? That I gave you two beautiful daughters, who you don't love anymore?"

"Who says I don't... No, *listen!* What I'm trying to tell you is that you care more about the house—and all that crap in it—than you ever cared about us!"

Jillian's fist hit the door so hard it banged against Scott's head.

"Ouch! Fuck it, Jillian!"

"No, fuck *you,* Scott. I cared enough to leave school and go to work, so you could get your MBA—which led to that cushy job you have. Not to mention that over-upholstered assistant you're sleeping with—"

He wrenched the door open again, but leaned into the doorjamb so she couldn't push it against him again. "Leave Victoria out of this, Jill. If things had been right at home, I wouldn't be here now, would I? And as for my job, I worked hard to get it and to keep it—" He was yelling so hard, she was sure he'd bust a vein. "—while you were...well, you know what you were doing!"

"What? What is that supposed to mean?"

"Cut the Mother Teresa crap. You don't think I'm playing the hard-ass for nothing, do you? I know you were using me, too, all those years."

"Scott, seriously. I don't know what the hell you're talking about!"

"Don't worry, your lawyer will soon have 'those details,' too. He can fill you in on them. In the meantime, if you insist on holding on to the Munster Mansion, why don't you get off your ass and get a job?"

"Doing what?"

"Hey, from what I remember, you were a good waitress once. I'm sure someone will hire you." With that, he slammed the door.

How dare he.

No matter how hard she rapped on the door, he wouldn't reopen it.

A third neighbor stuck her head out of her apartment. "I've called the police. Fair warning."

Jillian nodded. Then she ran down the hall, toward the elevator.

She didn't stop running until she got to her SUV. To do so, she had to pass his car first.

That's when the fun really began.

The first hit to his Porsche crushed the driver's side door.

Then, she rear-ended the car, but the damage was so negligible that she went back and tried it again.

The third hit, also on the rear, was so fast and so loud that she was sure his engine hadn't survived it. Hell, the collision had torn off her bumper and smashed a headlight, so she must have done some major damage to his car as well.

She took the drive home at around ten miles an hour because she hadn't counted on wrecking her SUV that night.

Her car gave out two blocks from Clarisse's house. When Clarisse answered the door, she grabbed her sleeping girls and said goodnight as quickly as she could, and prayed she didn't give the appearance that anything was wrong. She waited until Clarisse closed the door before placing them in the ugly old used stroller she had found on Craigslist. The stroller was harder to push uphill than her last one, but too bad. For now it would have to do, since it was the only way to get back home.

It was still *their* home.

As long as she could find a way to pay for it.

Come hell or high water, she would.

CHAPTER EIGHT

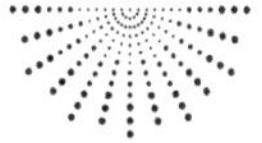

Wednesday, 19 September

So, this is how the one percent lives, Jade thought, as she eavesdropped on two Threesies mothers. They nod. They smile. They talk about the weather.

On this balmy September in San Francisco, it was the safest subject possible, especially for the Onesies moms who were competing against each other.

Thus far, what they had to do was simple: attend the meet-ups and make as many friends as possible. Within the group, the task of providing healthy snacks was being rotated. Jade's turn was on Friday, and her stomach was already in knots over it.

Brady had laughed when he saw her proposed list. "Fruit Roll-Ups? Are you serious?"

"What's wrong with that? It's made from real fruit, right? I mean, how much shredded carrots and celery mush can those poor kids eat?"

"Jade, doll, it's loaded with sugar. Not to mention all those preservatives!"

"I lived on this stuff growing up," she said. "It didn't hurt me any."

He shook his head as he left the room.

She wondered if he'd heard her crying.

Jade's first meet-up had taken place last Wednesday. Already it seemed like a thousand years ago.

She'd done exactly what Brady had directed her to do: she had smiled benignly, and only spoke if someone asked her a question. Unfortunately, most of the questions were about Oliver. They'd asked about the little things a mother should know about her child, but Jade hadn't been around to observe Oliver herself. Each time she made up an answer, her cheeks got hot as she worried if they were on to the fact that she was a fraud.

Worse, a deadbeat mom.

Before her second meeting that Friday, Brady had given her a cheat sheet. She was proud of the fact that she hadn't needed to rely on it, because she had spent Wednesday night and all day Thursday scrutinizing everything she could about her son—how well he walked, the words he could say, what he liked to eat, the sound of his laugh, the way he pursed his lips as he fell asleep.

The way he bounced whenever Brady came into view.

She knew the feeling.

Today, even in Alta Plaza Park, the wind had taken the day off, allowing the sun to toast the air. She smiled and waved at Lorna, who was strolling Dante toward her and Oliver. Together the women made their way to the bench where the other Onesies had congregated. Jade truly liked Lorna, and not just because Brady insisted she be nice to the Connaughts. Lorna was nice to everyone, even the catty Onesies like Chakra and Kelly.

She could tell Lorna liked to talk to her, too. Not that Kelly gave them much chance to do so. She seemed to want to snuggle up close to Lorna, to talk about Bettina. Some of the questions she asked were obnoxious: Were they close? Did they hang together a lot? Did Matt get along with Bettina's husband, Art?

What a nosy bee-hatch!

Lorna certainly seemed to be on to her little game, because she was good at changing the subject.

Another reason she liked Lorna was because she answered Jade's timid questions about the club and its members honestly, without any bullshit.

Like now. As the two women strolled past the picnic table where the Foursies moms had taken over, Jade overheard one mother say to another, "Anton started solids at six months, and was potty-trained at eight months. It's a shame your little Seth was so much slower to develop. Maybe that's why, now that he's four, he's not quite grasping the concept of Pottermore. Anton is a Ravenclaw. I am *so* proud of him."

Jade would have found the woman's boast more

believable if the supposedly smarter of the four-year-olds in question hadn't been dipping his tongue into a handful of sand while his mother was bragging about him. Despite this, both boys seemed happy and healthy as they played.

"My goodness, does it really matter if something happens for your kid a month or two earlier than the next kid?" Jade asked Lorna. "They all get around to the same milestones eventually, right?"

For some strange reason, that question wiped the smile completely off Lorna's face. "If you're a mom, every milestone makes you feel as if you've done at least one thing right. And if you're an insecure mom, there will always be something to boast about. So I'm guilty as charged." She shrugged. "But you're right. We all get to the same place eventually."

If only Lorna sounded as if she believed that herself.

ALLY AND JILLIAN HAD ALREADY STAKED OUT A METAL bench, which had been warmed by the sun. Not just warm, but hot. Jade found that out the hard way when she felt the burn on the back of her thighs. She regretted having worn her short shorts for just that reason.

Well, that and because the women who made up the PHM&T applications committee were doing a piss poor job at pretending not to stare at her.

When Bettina got up to walk over, Jade's heart skipped a beat. Brady had warned her that the shorts made her look slutty. If she got kicked out after just three meetings —even before the vote-off—he'd be so angry with her.

All eyes followed Bettina as she walked over to their bench. The conversation between Ally and Jillian about the girls and their favorite dolls stopped mid-sentence.

Bettina nodded to all of them, but she only had eyes for Jade. "Do you have a moment?" Bettina's tone was very serious.

Jade nodded warily and vowed to burn the shorts the very minute she got home. Worse yet, Bettina was going to ream her out in front of the others.

"The admissions committee has noted that you have excellent taste! Would you like to accompany me in lining up the Halloween Contest prizes from some of our more generous local merchants?"

"*Me?* Go…with you?" Jade couldn't believe her ears. She couldn't wait to tell Brady. He'd be ecstatic!

"It shouldn't be too obtrusive on your overall schedule. We only need eleven prizes: five boy prizes, one for each age group; and then five girl prizes, same criteria. Also, we'll need a Grand Prize. We could cover Chestnut Street in an hour on one day and Union Street another. On a third day, we'll hit the Fillmore district. Needless to say, your participation will count in your overall score. So, what do you say?"

"Of course! Any day you want!"

"Super. Why don't we meet at the Grove Cafe at eleven tomorrow morning? Feel free to bring Oliver along. Having the little ones with us always makes a great impression on the merchants. And he is *such* a handsome little guy!"

Jade nearly leaped off the bench to give Bettina a hug, then remembered her shorts and thought better of it.

The other Onesie moms tried to hide their disappointment, but it was all too clear what they were thinking: *Was Bettina already playing favorites?*

Jade certainly hoped so.

She looked down at her little son. He had already wormed his way out of his sweater and was deeply involved in some sandbox antics, taking a cup filled with sand and tossing it over one of his toy cars until it was completely buried. This process had Addison and Amelia squealing. Even that constant whiner, Quest, and Kelly's little bully, Wills, were both following him. By the time Ally's little girl, Zoe, joined in, it looked like a miniature conga line.

One of the twins (was it Amelia, or Addison? she could never tell them apart) grabbed Oliver's sweater, which had been tossed to one side, and threw it outside the sand lot. Jade laughed off Ally's apologies and ran after it. When she reached down for it, she noticed something odd: the collar held a tiny metal clasp, which was blinking green.

Why, that son of a bitch.

Jade scanned the streets surrounding the park. Yes, there he was, on the Steiner side.

If Brady wants to play I Spy, he should ditch the red Ferrari, she thought.

She almost smiled and waved but thought better of it. She'd wait for the right time, and the right place, to make him pay for his distrust.

She walked back toward the sand lot where Oliver was holding court with his newfound friends. If only he and Dante were doing a better job at bonding. Because she felt sorry that the little Connaught boy was being so shy, Jade handed another cup to Dante, but he just let it drop to the sand.

Then he stared at it as it lay there in front of him.

"He's just tired," Lorna smiled over at Jade. "We had a late night."

Jade nodded. Still, she couldn't help but think, *How is this kid going to make it through the competition? Even though he's Bettina's nephew, there just ain't no way…*

BRADY WAS SITTING IN THE LIVING ROOM, WAITING FOR JADE when she got home. The minute Oliver went down for his nap, Brady grilled her on every little detail. Which kids played with Oliver? If a kid didn't play with him, why not? What did the moms talk about? Had she said anything to upset anyone? Had Bettina singled her out for anything?

"Bettina invited me to go with her to find prizes for the winners of the Halloween parade. Isn't that great?"

"Wow, way to go." He gave her a thumbs up.

Her smile turned to stone. "Doesn't that deserve a kiss?"

He nodded slowly. "Yeah… I guess."

"You act as if I've got cooties or something! You know what, forget about it. Besides, I told her I didn't have time for that kind of stuff, since I'm only getting paid for the three mornings—"

He shrugged. "No, you didn't."

"Oh yeah? How do you know what I did or didn't do?"

"Because…I mean, I know you wouldn't have been that rude."

"You're right. I'm not rude. At least not as rude as you, who bugs his own son!" She glared at him. "Admit it, Brady. You already know everything that goes on at the meet-ups."

"What do you mean?" He'd tried to sound so innocent, but Jade had picked up on a habit of his—he blinked when he lied—and he was blinking now.

"I found the bug you planted on Ollie. In here." She tossed the jacket at him. "And I saw you in your car, watching us. What are you afraid of? That I might do a strip tease in the middle of the park?"

"No! Nothing like that. It's just that—well, through this initiation period, we have to be super good."

"I'm good all the time," she said with a naughty purr.

"That's not what I meant. The point I'm trying to make is—"

She had shut him up with a kiss.

Someday he'd kiss her first. She was sure of it.

Maybe on that same day he'd take the bug off Ollie's jacket.

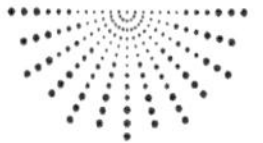

CHAPTER NINE

Thursday, 20 September
9:15 a.m.

"Scott did what? He dumped you?"

Jillian put a finger to her lips. "Mother, hush! The girls don't know yet."

"He was gone so often, I'm sure they barely know him anyway."

Jillian frowned. "That's a cruel thing to say."

"Oh, don't play holier-than-thou with me. You can't tell me you haven't thought the same thing a million times yourself."

For once, her mother was right. If only she could be right and nice at the same time.

"Ha! So that hoity-toity stick-in-the-mud you married turned out just like your father." Beverly's satisfied smirk grated on Jillian. "I guess it's right what they always say: 'Girls marry their daddies.'"

"Scott is nothing like Dad was." For one thing, Scott was a teetotaler, ergo the odds of him dying of cirrhosis of the liver were slim to none.

The last thing Jillian wanted was to get into an argument with her mother when she should be psyching herself up about the job interview with a restaurant in the Financial District. It was far enough away from the Marina and Pacific Heights that she shouldn't run into any PHM&T members.

It was time to change the subject. "So, you don't mind watching the girls while I take your car to go on this interview? The ad said to show up by ten o'clock. I'm guessing I'll be home by eleven at the latest."

"Not this time." The tone in her mother's voice said it all: *Don't expect me to do this anymore.*

The SUV would be back from the garage by tomorrow morning. She'd found a credit card Scott must have forgotten about, that they'd taken out in her name alone, and put its humongous repair bill on it—along with that week's grocery run. But she'd be reaching her limit soon if a more permanent settlement didn't force him into paying their expenses.

"They'll be good girls," Jillian promised. "They keep themselves busy—"

"Yeah, well too bad they can't change their own diapers and make my martinis."

Jillian countered with a weak smile. "That will

happen, soon enough, but not before lunch. They're smart girls. They're already growing up too quickly."

"Ha! You don't have to tell me! You were out of the house the minute you turned eighteen, like it was on fire or something."

That's because I had to get away from you, Jillian thought. *I was too afraid of turning into you...*

As if reading her mind, Beverly shrugged. "That's okay. You'll see. These two will do the same to you and leave you as soon as they can. Just like that asshole, Scott."

Without saying another word, Jillian ran out of the house.

BY THE TIME SHE GOT TO CLAXTON RESTAURANT, SHE'D wiped away most of the mascara that had pooled around her red-rimmed eyes. There were fifteen applicants waiting to be interviewed. When she finally got her turn with the manager, it was already a little after noon.

Her mother would be livid.

Then again, maybe the girls had caught on to how she liked her martinis.

With plush chairs, intimate alcoves, low lighting, and a straight-on view of the Bay Bridge, the place was elegant and appealing. The menu was eclectic and experimental.

It had to be in order to command thirty-dollars an entrée and more.

The restaurant was filling up, so the manager was conducting the interviews in an empty party alcove. He glanced from her to her application and back again. "It says here that you worked at The Dining Room in The Ritz Carlton. That closed, like, a bazillion years ago."

"In '05. I was there for six years prior to that—"

"Yeah, that was the point I was making. I'm wondering if you can still carry a tray."

What, is he kidding? I carry a twenty-two-pound toddler on each arm.

She laughed so hard that despite the fact she hadn't let him in on the joke, he actually cracked a smile, too.

Just then a waitress passed by carrying a tray laden with martinis. Jillian jumped up and patted her on the shoulder. Pointing at her tray, she asked sweetly, "May I?"

The woman looked at the manager, who hesitated before nodding. Jillian hoisted it shoulder height and did a turn around the room before setting it down in front of him with a grin.

All drinks accounted for, and not a drop was spilled.

"Okay, yeah. You made your point. We can start you at lunches, Sunday through Thursday. Minimum wage and tips, and you'll tip out the bus staff and bartenders. On a good day, you can expect to walk with one-ten."

Jillian pumped the air with her fist. Until she figured out that it meant missing the Monday and Wednesday PHM&T meet-ups.

"Oh…wait! That schedule won't work for me. I have a

standing engagement on Mondays and Wednesdays. But I can do nights."

That brought a smirk to the manager's face. "You can work up to nights if you prove yourself on the lunch shift. The only other shift I can offer is strictly weekends. That's two days versus five."

One-hundred-and-ten dollars times two days was only two-hundred-and-twenty dollars a week, eight hundred and eighty dollars a month. That would barely make a dent in her overhead. Jillian shrugged. "Can you throw in a Tuesday shift every now and then?"

"Maybe."

"How long will it take for me to get on nights?"

"Maybe a month."

She nodded, and they shook hands.

She could hold on until Tom Lutz could squeeze more than a monthly mortgage payment out of Scott. The permanent settlement was going in front of the judge sometime in the first week of November.

She'd be saying lots of prayers until then.

11: 12 a.m.

"Why have you been avoiding me?"

Brady hadn't expected to find Madame Ovary standing on his doorstep. He looked up and down the block before grabbing her wrist and pulling her inside the house.

"You shouldn't have just shown up here! What if Jade had been home?"

"Oh, quit panicking. Jade's with Bettina, hitting up merchants for the Halloween prizes. We both know that. Hell, it was my idea that she take Jade along. They'll be gone for two hours, at a minimum. Bettina is like a Canadian Mountie. She doesn't stop until she gets what she wants, and in this case, all her bullshit tchotchkes. I, on the other hand, want *you*." She slammed him against the wall before grinding into him.

It wasn't easy talking with her tongue crammed down his throat. "Yes! Well, I think we should cool things for the time being. You know, until this competition thing is over."

That stopped her cold. With suspicion in her eyes, she pulled away. "What, are you crazy? No sex…for the next six months?"

"I just thought that if, for any reason, you felt it might put you in a compromising position—"

She put his hands on her breasts. "*This* is a compromising position. And this—" She cupped his cock with her hands. "And this." In no time at all, she'd yanked open his jeans and dropped to her knees.

He struggled to find his voice while she went down on him. When he did, his words came out in a gasp. "I—I really don't think this is a great idea… Ouch! *What the hell*—"

She glared up at him. "Sorry about that. I grind my

teeth when I'm upset. And I get upset when I think someone is trying to get rid of me."

"Trying to…*what?* Get rid of you? No! Not at all!" He turned quickly to zip up his pants.

"Good, because I'd hate to think you only like me because I get to vote in the competition."

She started up to the bedroom without even a glance back.

There was nothing he could do but follow.

Afterward, he made sure she picked up all her clothes. Especially her panties. The last thing he needed was for Jade to be upset at him and leave him high and dry.

1:35 p.m.

Jade came home floating on a cloud. "Bettina loved everything I chose!" she informed Brady proudly. "As a thank you, she wants us to join her and her husband, Art, for dinner. What do you think of that?"

Brady nodded grudgingly. Jade scored big time with the Chief Executive Mommy. He had to give her that. Maybe they had nothing to worry about after all.

"Look! Aren't these cute?" She pointed to the array of toys she'd already spread out onto the living room floor, everything from learning toys to dolls and super hero action figures for the Foursies and Fivesies. "And I found this one at the cute little children's store on Webster, called Bubble!" She held up a black onesie scrawled with the slogan I ♥

MARINA CHICKS. "Wouldn't Ollie look great in it? I hope he wins it. Of course, I offered to wrap all the gifts, too! Gotta keep those Bettina Badges coming, right? Want to help?"

"Don't call him Ollie. Never. Ever. Okay? And I don't have time to help. I was invited to speak at the D: All Things Digital conference downtown."

He was lying. Yes, he was going to the conference, but no, he wasn't speaking, just taking in a panel or two. Between her and Madame Ovary, and all the gossip and mama drama he heard through the bug on Oliver's jacket, he needed to get away from women, at least for one night.

"Oh...kay." Her nod was accompanied by a frown. "Well, maybe we can get a babysitter, and I can go with you."

"Nah. Trust me. All that tech stuff is boring. Just stay home and relax. You've earned it."

Before she made a bigger issue of it, he bounded up the stairs for a shower.

He could smell Madame Ovary on himself. The scent was so strong he was surprised Jade hadn't noticed.

Thank goodness for that.

2:22 p.m.

"Ellis went home early! He has food poisoning!" Ally's office assistant, Jen, hissed from the doorway. "He thinks he ate some bad ahi at lunch. I swear, those Midwest guys can't hold their sushi."

"Well, he can't blame that on me, too." Ally shook her

head. The news was enough to shift her gaze from her computer screen, where she had been perusing Foot Fetish's latest P&L statement. Last month's sales had somehow dropped off a cliff, and she couldn't figure out why.

Ellis claimed that her latest designs "hadn't quite caught the zeitgeist," as he had so pompously put it. He was wrong. The company's Twitter followers and Facebook fans had been ecstatic over the new collection. In fact, they'd been claiming that they couldn't get enough of these new shoes—

"—So, BI corporate offices called and said you have to take his place on the D: All Things Digital Conference panel. The one about retailing successfully through apps."

"What? I can't do that! I have to get back to Zoe!"

"Ally, this is *D: All Things Digital!* Look, if you're not going, then *you* need to call the chairman of the board."

But of course Ally would go.

It was part of her pact with the devil.

Ally shrugged. "Okay, It's at four o'clock, at Moscone, right? Then I guess I better call my nanny and tell her she's got massive overtime coming her way." Ally looked down at her old jeans and the faded tank top she wore under a jacket that had seen better days. In other words, it was mom wear.

Upon hearing her long, anguished sigh, Jen pointed at the Saks Fifth Avenue across the street. "Designer sale. Just sayin'."

"Really? Thank God for small miracles! Okay, call the

chairman and tell him I've got it covered." She was out the door in a flash.

4:01 p.m.

Ally gave great anecdote.

Like the one about the time the cargo container from China was filled with sex slaves as opposed to open-toed sandals.

And how long it took to discover that Foot Fetish's very first app was linked to an S&M site instead of their online store.

And how, as a single mom, she'd given birth to her daughter on the same day she closed the acquisition by BI.

And in the Bottega Veneta cocktail dress she'd found at the sale, all of these incidents flowed trippingly off her tongue because she knew she was the sexiest woman in the room.

In all honesty, she was the only woman in a room filled with guys who actually looked up every now and then from their computers in order to laugh out loud with her.

It was during the Q&A that she saw him: Brady Pierce.

At first, she hadn't recognized him. Maybe that was because the last time she'd seen him, he'd had a baby on his shoulders.

Without the toddler, he was even better looking than she'd remembered.

I can see what Jade sees in him, she thought.

Obviously he'd already placed her, because his eyes never left her face.

That know-it-all grin never left his face, either.

Then, the possible reason for his smile hit Ally like a ton of bricks: *Oh, hell. He now knows I'm still involved with the company. He can use that to get me ousted from the club.*

As if reading her mind, he raised his hand. The moderator pointed to him, warning the crowd that it would be the last question of the session. "Ms. Thornton, has it been difficult running a multi-billion dollar company *and* being a full-time parent?"

She wondered if her face were as red as her new dress. At least she had the smarts to pause before answering, "I'm working on an app for that."

That got the biggest laugh of all.

Ally was the only one in the room who wasn't laughing.

"I KNOW WHAT YOU'RE THINKING," BRADY SAID WHEN HE finally caught up to her.

It was easy for him to do, considering his legs were very long, and her heels were too tall.

She stopped short. "Oh yeah? What's that?"

"You're wondering if I'm going to out you to the club. Am I right?"

"Of course. Six families. Four slots. Do the math."

God, you're so beautiful, Brady thought. Even when you're vulnerable. *Especially now, when your back is against the wall, and you're trying so hard to be strong…*

"How about a drink? We can walk over to the St. Regis. It's got a great bar."

"You're kidding, right?"

"No, I'm not." He looked her in the eye. "We all have our dirty little secrets."

"Oh yeah? What's yours?"

He shrugged. "You'll have to get me drunk to find out."

That brought a smile to her face. "Sure. If you're spilling your guts, then I'm buying."

Even in heels, she kept pace with him all the way to the St. Regis.

She must have needed that drink as badly as he did.

11:41 p.m.

He was surprised by how easy he found it to divulge his own bizarre machinations regarding the Pacific Heights Moms & Tots Club.

He told her how he'd met Jade at a strip club, and it was lust at first sight; how, when Jade had told him she was pregnant, his heart had sunk, but he knew he'd stand by his kid, no matter what; how, when Oliver was only five months old, Jade had put her so-called career ahead of their son's health, and their baby's raging fever had landed Oliver in the hospital; and how, because of the club's rules forbidding dads' participation other than at their adult parties, he'd bitten the bullet and had invited Jade back into his life.

That's what happens when you let a pretty woman buy you a triple Johnny Walker Blue, he reasoned.

"She loves Ollie," Ally insisted. "It shows in everything she does for him."

Brady grimaced at the nickname. "It's *Oliver*. Yeah, yeah, I know she calls him that all the time. Someday I'll break her of the habit. And yes, I know she loves him. But…well, I never loved her."

Ally grinned as she patted his arm. "Love is like sand, isn't it? Shifting with time, but always there in some form. We never know what the future holds, do we?"

More of you, I hope. Right then and there, he could have kissed her.

Instead, he picked up the tab and walked her to her car.

"Mum's the word," he promised.

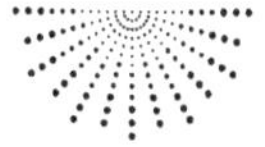

Monday, 8 October

"LADIES! LADIES! GATHER 'ROUND, PLEASE." BETTINA'S lilting declaration was more of a command than a pleasantry.

The mothers from the various groups within the club quit chattering and did as they were told.

"As we all know, Halloween is just around the corner, which means the PHM&T's annual Halloween party is as well."

The squeals and claps were to be expected, despite the fact that the members had been prepping for the event for weeks.

Unlike the probationary Onesies, who, until now, hadn't realized how big a deal it was.

"The rules are *strict.*" The emphasis on that last word

came with a laser-like gaze at the newbie Onesies, so they could gauge the importance the event would have on their survival in the club. "First, all costumes are handmade, by each child's mother. Be original, people! The mundane is abhorred, whereas the eclectic is celebrated! Second, all children must participate in the parade in order to be eligible for our wonderful prizes, which were chosen by one of our probationary Onesies, Jade Pierce…" Bettina's hand swept out toward Jade in a gesture of gracious inclusion, "…along with *moi*. So, yes, you *will* love them."

Again, not a mere statement, but a command.

The applause that accompanied her departure proved this.

Jillian slumped down on the bench. Between single parenting and almost two weeks of waiting tables, she was downright exhausted. Now she had to make the girls' costumes by hand, too? What she knew about sewing wasn't much more than how to thread a needle to sew on a button. Maybe she could put the girls in large white paper bags lined with a row of black buttons down the center, and they could come as snowmen.

Noting the look on her face, Ally gave her a gentle hug. "Oh, come on, it won't be that difficult to whip something up."

"Speak for yourself," Lorna murmured. Her face mirrored Jillian's worry. In anticipation of the event, she'd already spent a fortune on a miniature Sherlock Holmes outfit she'd found in a costume catalog. Knowing Bettina the way she did, she presumed the word "eclectic" meant the costumes had to be something no one else would have thought of—in other words, no ghosts, witches, Hulks or Iron Man costumes.

"I've got an idea." Ally turned to face them all. "Why not work on them together? There's no rule that says we can't. In fact, we can do it at my house. I'm into crafts, so if you have an idea of what you'd like to make, let me know. I'll see what kind of cloth and felt and feathers and buttons I've got in my stash. Everyone can come by after the meet-up next Monday."

"I'm in!" Lorna and Jillian said at the same time, then laughed together.

"Me, too," Jade said. For once, she felt close to the others—and not just because Brady would be pleased with her.

"I'll pass," Chakra declared with a sniff. "I'm sure whatever you've been holding in your basement is synthetic, not to mention covered in mold spores."

Ally shook her head to keep from lashing out. Her fabric stash came from the pristine design studio at Foot Fetish, not that the other women needed to know that.

"I've already ordered some bolts of organic cotton from India," Chakra said. "And I'll be making my own glue. That way it's non-toxic. And edible, in fact."

"Ah! So that explains it..." Ally muttered under her breath.

The others turned away to keep from laughing out

loud. Thank goodness the slight went right over Chakra's head.

Or maybe not.

"Gotta run!" Chakra growled. "Sally and I are diagramming the children's harvest of the PHM&T's communal garden. She can't do anything without me."

"We've noticed," Kelly said in mock innocence.

"Well, missy, there is something else that's been noticed—by the applications committee: your late attendance to meet-ups."

Seeing, Chakra's smirk, Kelly turned white.

As Chakra sauntered over to Sally's bench, Kelly muttered, "Well, she's certainly making herself indispensable to the committee. I guess that's one way to play the game."

The same thought had crossed everyone's mind at that exact moment: *How far do I have to go to win a slot?*

Kelly leaned over to Lorna and whispered, "What will you make for Dante's costume?"

Lorna shook her head. "To tell you the truth, I've got no idea."

"Me neither! But I've got one great idea, why don't we dress the boys alike? It would be *so* cute!"

Lorna didn't know how to tell Kelly that this was the last thing she'd want to do, but then she thought better of it. Other than gushing over Jade, Bettina hadn't been playing favorites.

Still, there was a reason Kelly was sitting there on the bench with the rest of them, so there must be a good reason why Bettina saw it fitting to have her old high school BFF around, despite her chronic tardiness.

Okay sure, why not dress the boys alike? Lorna wondered. It'll be a good bonding experience for both Dante and for me. Besides, it's like they say: keep your friends close and your enemies closer. I'm guessing Kelly is the former with Bettina as opposed to the latter. One thing *is for sure: if it turns out I'm wrong, she can't make Bettina hate me more than she already does.*

CHAPTER ELEVEN

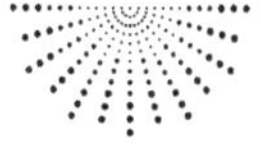

Monday, 15 October

"SORRY TO BOTHER YOU, ALLY." THE DREAD IN JEN'S VOICE released a trickle of sweat down Ally's back. "But Ellis is wondering if you'll be joining us for the strategy session that was scheduled for eleven o'clock today."

Confused, Ally stared down at her new cell phone. Maybe the reception was bad. "What? But it's Monday. My contract explicitly states that all meetings requiring my attendance will be held on either Tuesdays or Thursdays! He knows that."

Jen had called right as Ally was cleaning the remains of Zoe's breakfast from her high chair tray. She sighed as she perused the wall next to the chair, where Zoe had just smeared oatmeal in an attempt at mural art.

"DOCK!" the little girl stated proudly, despite the stain's six legs and two heads.

Ally forced her mouth into a smile. "Jen, put Ellis on the phone—*now*."

At least the on-hold music was somewhat apropos: Billy Joel, growling *My Life*.

"Ally! Top of the morning to you!" Ellis's fake attempt at cheeriness almost made Ally gag.

"Cut it out, Ellis. It will be anything but that if you dare break the contract and schedule meetings requiring my attendance on days which aren't covered by it."

"There are some decisions that need immediate attention! You know, Ally, not all of us have the luxury of being on the 'mommy track.'"

"Well, then maybe 'all of us' need to get a better attorney. Mine is wonderful. In fact, if he got wind of what you've just tried here, he'd be on the phone to Bracknell's chairman to remind them of the penalty for breaking the contract."

There was silence on the other end of the line. Ally imagined he was weighing the odds of winning at this psycho attempt at corporate cocksmanship against those of losing his job for costing Bracknell International a pretty penny.

"Tomorrow then? See if you can squeeze it into your schedule." She had her answer.

Before she could hear the click that told her he'd hung up on her, she threw her new cell phone onto the couch.

Zoe ran to retrieve it. Excited that she'd beat her mother to it, she tossed it into the sink—

Where it plopped into the soapy dishwater.

Ally buried her head in her hands. Maybe living without a cell phone wasn't such a bad idea.

At least until Zoe was four or so.

Wow, her aim is incredible! I wonder how old she has to be for softball league?

12:22 p.m.

Ally had outdone herself for what the Probationary Onesies were now calling "the costume workshop." Along with bolts in all shades and fabrics and textures, there were scissors, glue guns, glitter, plus tiny plastic jars of water paints, feathers, buttons, Styrofoam balls, and cardboard.

She'd also gone out of her way to get solid-colored one-piece footed pajamas in a rainbow selection of toddler sizes 12 to 24 months.

Lorna gave a long, low whistle. "I feel as if I've walked into Martha Stewart's workshop. This is incredible!" She picked up a footsie. "Smart thinking! These will cut our work in half."

Jillian nodded. "That's fine by me, since I've got to make two of them."

"Your daughters are adorable. Like two peas in a pod." Jade stroked Amelia's cheek while she slept. Thank goodness the workshop was taking place during all the toddlers' naptime. Jade froze then picked up two solid green footsies. "That's it! Why not make them peas in a pod?"

"Oh my God! What a great idea! I can paint these Styrofoam balls light green, and run them right beside the zipper, then layer felt onto their footsies, to make the pod. They'll have green felt hats, too, and *voila*!" Jillian grabbed a paintbrush and went to work.

In a few minutes, everyone was busy at work. Jade was putting stripes on a white footsie, the first step toward a little baseball outfit sporting the number 55—San Francisco Giants pitcher, Tim Lincecum.

Kelly and Lorna had decided on Robin Hood outfits.

When the doorbell rang, Ally was gluing peacock feathers on a turquoise footsie for Zoe's bird costume. She was surprised to see Brady standing on the other side of the door.

"Where's the party?" he asked.

"In here, to the left. Follow me."

He'd follow her to the ends of the earth if she'd let him.

In the meantime, he would admire her from afar.

For now anyway.

Although the other women waved at him, they were too wrapped up in their projects to notice Jade's joy as she threw herself into his arms.

Everyone but Ally, that is.

Jade's kiss was aimed at Brady's lips, but he jerked his head away, and the kiss landed on his chin instead.

She shrugged it off, but he could tell she was hurt.

Ally must have known, too, because she turned away too quickly, spilling the bottled water on the table beside her elbow.

"Damn, damn, damn," she muttered as she swabbed the spill with a dishcloth.

That's when Brady realized Ally would never do anything to hurt her new friend, Jade.

They were all in this together. Jade included.

He too wanted to let loose with a litany of curses, but he couldn't.

Just like he couldn't take Ally in his arms.

Or kiss her. Or tell her how she was everything he'd been looking for in a woman. Up until now, he'd let his dick or his brogrammer ego lead him to flashy, stacked women who were wowed by his money, his smarts, and his reputation for making them miserable.

Ally didn't want him to make her miserable. She just wanted to be his friend.

But that wasn't an option.

One way or another, he'd convince her of that.

But first he'd have to make Jade understand she was here for Oliver and not for him.

That wasn't going to be easy. But it was the only option she'd have, if she wanted to stay in Oliver's life.

CHAPTER TWELVE

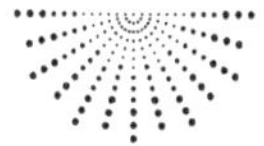

Monday, 22 October

IF YOU WERE TO ASK SALLY, CHAKRA WAS A DREAM COME true. Not only did she hoe, rake, compost, plant, fertilize, and water on command, but in Sally's timid mind, she'd also taken on the hardest job of all: Shaming the other moms into taking their designated shifts.

Granted, throwing that tomato at the Threesie mother who refused to weed the garden in brand new trousers was going a bit too far, but Chakra's sullen apology had been accepted (along with Sally's promise to babysit the woman's toddler on two separate occasions, *and* buy her a new pair of pants).

So Sally was heartbroken when, loading the gardening tools into the trunk of Chakra's Nissan Leaf electric car, she discovered the clear plastic sales bag containing little Quest's Halloween costume—and the purchase receipt.

She was still deciding whether it was worth covering for Chakra when Mallory walked up behind her. "Wow, this is a pretty big trunk for an electric car."

Sally almost jumped out of her skin before slamming the trunk lid.

Mallory whipped her hand away just in time. "Jesus, Sally! You broke my nail! What was that white thing in there anyway?"

"Nothing. Just…an old rug."

She was lying. It was a fleece lamb costume from some organic costume company based in Berkeley.

If Quest wore it to the parade, and Mallory recognized it and realized Sally had covered up the infraction, Sally would be just as dead to the club as Chakra.

This year, Halloween was turning out to be scary for all the wrong reasons.

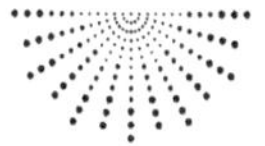

CHAPTER THIRTEEN

Wednesday, 24 October

IT WAS LORNA'S IDEA THAT THE ONESIES ATTEND AN IT'S Yoga mom-and-baby class in the Presidio as that morning's meet-up activity. As she watched the other mothers breathing and stretching with their toddlers to the directions murmured by the studio's instructor, she too breathed deeply. This event was exactly what she needed to solidify her place in the club.

Bettina had sent Mallory as her eyes and ears. Unfortunately, the way Mallory tapped her foot and clucked her tongue during the whole session was anything but relaxing. Not only that, Lorna didn't like the way Mallory was scrutinizing Dante. The scorn in Mallory's eyes as Dante groaned whenever Lorna tried to follow the instructor's gentle directive to stretch his leg, or lift his arm, was obvious. Whereas the other children laughed and cooed at being stretched and played with, Dante preferred that Lorna leave him be. To her dismay, her touch was shrugged off.

If Mallory weren't watching, she would have teared up. Instead, she smiled and laughed; all the while pretending Dante's actions were normal.

But she knew better.

It was a hollow victory when, afterward, all the other mothers gave Lorna a round of applause at the instructor's behest. The worst part was seeing the concern on the instructor's face as Dante covered his ears with his hands and started humming.

As the other women and their children flowed out of the room, the instructor laid her hand on Lorna's arm to hold her back. "Your son—Dante, isn't it?—such a sweet, handsome boy. I know his disorder must be challenging. Please feel free to bring him to one of our 'Yoga for the Special Child' classes—"

Lorna stared at the woman. "What? I don't get it."

The instructor's eyes deepened with the realization of Lorna's cluelessness. "Oh! I thought Dante's doctor may have referred you to our studio."

"No! I heard a few moms rave about your program, and I thought it would be nice for our moms and tots group. I think everyone was fine with it."

Everyone but Dante.

Lorna could tell the woman was thinking the very same thing.

At that moment, Lorna realized that Mallory was still in the studio, looking at the schedule posted on the wall. Had she overheard the conversation?

If so, that would ruin Dante's acceptance into the PHM&T Club, where everything was perfect. His rejection into the club would be just the start of all the sad, bad things that could happen to him. It could ruin his life.

She could never let that happen. Ever.

Clutching Dante to her chest, she walked out the door without another word to the woman.

I have to find out if something is wrong with him, she thought as she strapped Dante into his car seat. *No matter what it is, we'll deal with it…*

That woman mentioned a doctor who would know.

She waited until all the other mother's cars had cleared the parking lot—Mallory's included—before heading back inside, Dante in tow.

The instructor was making notes at the front desk. Her grin disappeared when she realized Lorna was back, and that she wasn't smiling.

"What did you mean when you said you had classes for 'special children'?" Lorna asked.

"We've developed a therapeutic yoga program for children with all kinds of developmental or learning disabilities: Autism, Cerebral Palsy, Attention Deficit Hyperactivity Disorder, and Downs Syndrome. Yoga has been proven to increase the body awareness of such children." The woman reached for a brochure and held it out to Lorna who hesitated to take it.

Could she be the right? Lorna thought. No, never…

Then why didn't he smile more? Why wasn't he more attentive when she talked to him?

She looked at her son. If the instructor was right, was she a bad mother for not realizing it earlier?

Lorna took it from the woman's hand. "You mentioned a doctor who works with children with—with those disorders. Who would that be?"

The woman opened the desk's drawer and pulled out a business card: *David Remfeld M.D. Pediatric Neurology*

She was relieved to see it wasn't her own pediatrician, since her niece, Lily, was also her patient, as were most of the children in the PHM&T Club.

This afternoon she'd call Dr. Remfeld's office for the first available appointment.

He would put all her qualms to rest.

Not that she had anything to worry about. Dante was perfect. Her little Renaissance man. *But just in case.*

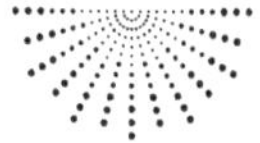

CHAPTER FOURTEEN

Tuesday, 30 October

Dr. Remfeld's office within the UCSF Pediatric Autism and Neurology Clinic was painted in calming tones of pale greens and blues. The furniture was casual and well upholstered, similar to what one would find in an upscale resort. Colorful learning toys were scattered about in order to entice the children whose parents waited anxiously for assurance that their children were all right.

Had her mind not been so shocked at the results of Dante's tests, had her heart not been breaking from the doctor's assessment—that Dante would never feel joy or love like other children—Lorna might have certainly been more appreciative of the setting.

Well, now she knew why Dante was oblivious to it as well.

As the doctor explained that Dante's tests had indicated autism, she realized all her hopes and dreams for him would never come true.

"He's too young for us to determine the severity of his disorder." Dr. Remfeld's voice was soft and soothing for the life sentence he'd just delivered. "We'll test him every three months. And there are simple exercises you can do with him that may strengthen his cognitive responses. These only improve his rote skills, but still—"

Lorna nodded, as if to show she understood what he was saying.

Did it matter? The bottom line was Dante didn't belong.

He'd never belong. Anywhere.

She didn't know how she was going to break that news to Matt.

Of course once she did, he'd tell Eleanor, his rock, his place for solace.

When that happened, Dante would no longer be her favorite.

And Bettina would use Dante's affliction to kick them out of the club; to have him ostracized in the eyes of the other mothers and children.

Lorna couldn't let that happen.

Now she had the most important reason in the world to stay on Bettina's good side: for Dante's sake.

She'd keep the news to herself. Even Matt couldn't know. For now, anyway.

She'd wait for just the right time to tell him.

The thought that one could ever presume there might be a "right time" to hear your child had a neurological disorder that would keep him from living a normal life had her convulsing with laughter. By the time her hysteria gave way to tears and curses, a nurse was knocking on the door asking if there was anything she could do to help.

Lorna already knew the answer to that.

CHAPTER FIFTEEN

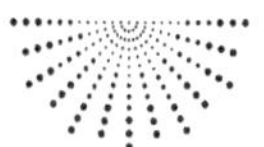

Wednesday, 31 October

As far as Bettina was concerned, the Halloween Party was an unmitigated disaster.

First off, most of the costumes were unimaginative. Trite even. If you've seen one fairy, you've seen them all, right? And not any one fairy can win a prize, or the others would expect one, too.

As the PHM&T group paraded along with the rest of the annual Union Street Halloween festival, it became obvious that the most imaginative costumes were those of the Probationary Onesies. Except for Quest's little lamb get-up. It might have been organic and eco-friendly, but it was also *boring*.

Bettina winced at the thought that their successes

would make it even more difficult tomorrow when one of them would have to be cast aside.

If it were up to her, the loser would be Jade.

Not only did she have an awful sense of style, she was unimaginably naïve. How could she actually believe that Bettina liked her?

While it was fun to taunt the others with the favoritism she showed the Pierce woman, the simple fact of the matter was that snuggling up to Jade allowed her to get as close as possible to Brady Pierce.

That way Art could also get close to Brady. Maybe even close enough to manage his money for him. In a financial management firm like Lichman Parker Bowles, bringing in the Pierce estate could make the difference between junior and senior partner.

She nudged Art as Jade came into sight. "That's the wife! The woman in the black cat suit." She almost added, "The one that looks like an Avenger slut," but since half the women out tonight would be in some version of that same costume, she thought better of it.

Art scanned the marchers. His smirk made it obvious that he had found Jade. "Scarlett Johansson, where have you been all my life? She can avenge me anytime!"

Bettina didn't nudge next, but poked. Hard. Between two ribs. "Don't blow this, Art. We need the money too badly."

"If you really think so, then don't accept every invitation you get to sit on some charity committee. Those donations and ten-person tables are breaking us. Not to mention the cost for every new designer gown you buy for those shindigs."

"Don't blame me! Those charities are how you meet clients, remember? Now if you could only keep your hands off their wives…"

She stopped, only because something caught her eye: Dante's Robin Hood costume. It looked exactly the same as the one on Kelly's little Wills.

Art must have seen her, too, because he did a double take. "Hey, isn't that Kelly Bryant, your old girlfriend from Lick?"

"Yep, that's Kelly Bryant *Overton* all right." Bettina prayed her voice wasn't trembling.

"I didn't know she was in your club."

"She's a Onesie probie. Gee, I'm sure I'd mentioned it." She hadn't, but that was beside the point.

How could Lorna do that to her? *The traitor.*

"No, I would have remembered if you had." Art's laugh was half-hearted at best. "And by the looks of it, she and Lorna are buddy-buddy."

That bitch.

When her application had come in, Bettina thought she was strong enough to put up with her shenanigans. Now, she wasn't so sure.

She's always wanted what I have! It's just not fair.

But no, not this time. I'm going to have so much fun crushing her.

She felt a tap on her shoulder. She turned to say hello to Dr. Remfeld who ran one of UCSF's children's clinics.

She'd forgotten which one, there were so many of them over there, and she sat on the boards of at least three.

Maybe Art was right. They were much too generous. Saying no didn't give her the same high as saying yes, but it would have to do. At least until he landed the Pierce estate.

THE PARADE SHOULD HAVE BEEN A HAPPIER EVENT, BUT FOR the Probationary Onesies there was too much riding on it.

For Ally, it didn't help that Barry showed up to see Zoe in the parade—holding hands with Christian. She didn't have the heart to scold him for forgetting that he was playing her beard in this little charade. At the same time, Ally prayed Joanna didn't see them when they kissed Zoe and told her she was the prettiest peacock ever, and she squealed, "My dadas!"

LORNA WAS HAPPY TO SEE HER MOTHER-IN-LAW, ELEANOR, standing next to Matt, waving at her and Dante. Well, Eleanor was waving at Dante anyway. But Bettina's scowl was a bit disconcerting.

What have I done now? Lorna wondered.

Then she saw him: Dr. Remfeld. And he was talking to Bettina.

Lorna's heart sank in her chest.

BECAUSE HER LAST CUSTOMER LINGERED OVER DESSERT, Jillian's shift ran late, and she and the girls almost didn't get to walk with the Onesies who were up at the front of the parade. That would have been a disaster. The way Mallory glared at her, she presumed she'd blown their chances. All for a six-dollar tip.

WITH JADE'S BUDDING FRIENDSHIP WITH BETTINA, BRADY thought he didn't have a worry in the world—until Madame Ovary inched her way through the crowd and pinched his ass. Just then, Jade looked up. When Brady saw the strange, sad look on her face, all he could think was, *Oh shit…*

JADE FELT SURE SHE'D LOCKED UP ONE OF THE COVETED SLOTS —until she looked out into the crowd and saw *one of her customers from the Condor Club standing right next to Bettina.* What the hell was he doing here? And now he was looking right at her—and whispering something in Bettina's ear!

Instinctively, Jade looked over at Brady. Why was he frowning at her?

THE ONESIES GIRL WINNER WAS A LEGACY'S DAUGHTER. ALLY and Jillian shrugged away their disappointment. Zero Bettina Badges there. All they could do was bide their time until tomorrow to hear if they were still in the club after whatever slights they'd given Bettina or any of the PHM&T's applications committee.

The Onesies boy winner was an easy call: Oliver Pierce.

Lorna's disappointment must've been evident, because Bettina whispered in her ear: "You cut your odds in half when you teamed up with Kelly. What the hell were you thinking? All I can say is if you get voted down, don't blame me."

Oh yeah, Lorna thought. Who else would I blame?

Ironically, the first name that popped into her head was *Kelly*.

She wished she knew why.

CHAPTER SIXTEEN

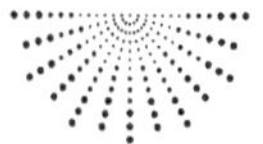

Thursday, 1 November

"Omigod!" Mallory crowed. "So many infractions! Look, I've done a chart."

The names were listed horizontally along the top with the date and infraction beneath it.

"That's stupid," Joanna said. "Half of those are in your imagination, Mallory."

"Yeah, agreed," Kimberley said. "Besides, you can't count 'brought fruit roll-ups as a snack' the same as 'has shown up late at least six times.' I mean, come on already, at least *grade* the level of infraction."

She had a point. Jade's fruit roll-ups had been worth a week of chortles. But Kelly's lateness—which could run more than thirty minutes each time—was a slap in the collective faces of the club's members.

Sally turned pale as she thought of Chakra's infraction. If her name was already on Mallory's chart and Sally didn't speak up about it first, Mallory would accuse her of a cover-up.

And enjoy doing so.

Then Sally would be banished from the club, too.

She had just started to scan the chart for Chakra's name when Mallory snatched it away. "Grade them? No way! The worst probationer is obvious, trust me. It's—"

Before she had could say another word, Sally shouted, "Chakra bought Quest's costume! I...I saw the bag and receipt...and everything. I just wanted it noted, for the record."

Everyone turned to stare at her.

Mallory shook her head in awe. "Wow. Didn't see *that* one coming. Although I did think it strange that a PETA member would dress her kid like a little lamb, and then not drench the costume in red paint or something."

Aw hell, Sally thought. I outted her for nothing?

Bettina couldn't believe her ears. If Chakra's infraction was by far the most serious, then her one chance to get rid of the woman who was making her life a laughing stock was about to go out the window.

She couldn't let that happen.

"I think Kimberley has a great point," Bettina said. She snatched the infraction chart out of Mallory's hand, then threw it back at her. "Mallory, read each probationer's demerits, and we'll each grade them, on a scale of one to three, three being the most egregious."

Mallory smiled. "Everyone, grab a paper and pencil! We'll start with Jillian. During the Onesies' inauguration gala, she broke Rule Number 1443 of the PHM&T Membership Manual: 'No one will solicit another member for the purchase of anything.' I personally witnessed her selling her stroller to another mother! What does she think we're running here, a second-hand baby gear flea market?"

Bettina shrugged. "Granted, she hadn't received her manual until after she sold the stroller. And she *did* give part of the proceeds to our fundraiser. Nevertheless, the transgression will count against her. These clueless newbies! Let's see what other demerits she's earned, shall we?"

Mallory marked the sheet with a check. "Then there was the time she called to say her twins were sick with some contagion, but that very night she left them at another member's house so she could go out on the town with her husband! I guess they weren't so sick after all..."

CHAPTER SEVENTEEN

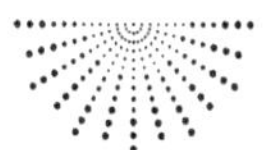

Friday, 2 November

IT WAS A GRAY MORNING. OVERCAST WAS NORMAL FOR THE start of San Francisco's rainy season, but today was bleaker still for the Probationary Onesies as they awaited news of their fate.

They gathered around the designated picnic table in Alta Plaza Park. Lorna found it ironic that it was the same table where, some three months ago, Dante's Pampers had flown out of her hand. So much had happened since then.

At least Bettina wouldn't beat around the bush. Her justice would be quick and cruel.

Even if it were toward her own nephew.

Each of them felt the same, and had come to accept the possibility that today they may be the one ousted.

"In reviewing your participation, I have to say that I found more to be dismayed about than I'd expected." Bettina paused dramatically. "But I'm sure that for those of you who will be joining us over the next few months, you'll finally find your rhythm in our mother-and-child symphony and strike a few chords that resonate with the rest of us."

She scanned each face, slowly. "If you leave here today, know it's because you've broken our trust in such a way that we could not just forgive and forget. To do so would cause the biggest scandal this club has ever seen—"

The probationers' winces were plainly visible.

Bettina had hoped that would be the case.

"—and it would not be fair to our members to suffer through it, because of what you did—"

The intake of breath could have been mistaken for one more gale force wind blowing through the park.

"Chakra, you may go."

Chakra?

Ally, Jillian, Jade, and Lorna couldn't believe their ears.

So, that was the "big scandal" that would cast ruin on the club and its members?

Bettina was rattling on about Chakra's costume: something about it being store bought…

Chakra's goodbye to the group was swifter than Bettina's dressing down. It was a one-finger salute, and a quote from Shakespeare: "A plague on all your houses!"

Bettina made a note to herself to have the garden tilled

under, just in case Chakra retaliated with natural pesticides.

Perhaps they'd move the garden to an undisclosed location.

Better yet, they'd take the children to the Pier One Farmer's Market instead. The mothers would rejoice because it provided less opportunity for the children to dirty their clothes.

A storm lurched out of the sky and over the park, breaking up the meet-up.

"Kelly, would you mind staying a bit?" Bettina's voice was smooth as honey. "I'd like to have a word with you, in private."

Kelly smiled and nodded.

Jade wondered, Is she Bettina's new favorite? If so, is it because the Condor Club client informed Bettina about my time as a pole dancer?

But that can't be. If Bettina knew about it, then I would have been the one who was let go!

For some reason, he hadn't.

Relief flooded her like a cold sweat. Suddenly she felt light-headed and happy. "Hey, why not come over to my house for hot cocoa," Jade suggested to the others.

Ally, Jillian, and Lorna were feeling just as euphoric. They'd survived the cut! Their secrets were safe.

For now.

Their cars pulled up at Jade and Brady's house around the same time. A strange car, a Lexus, was in the driveway.

Maybe not so strange. At least, Lorna thought she recognized it. "That car belongs to a PHM&T applications committee member. I forget which one, but I recognize the license plate: 'Gr8Mama'."

No one wanted to say out loud what they were thinking, or why: *Had the application committee learned that they'd ousted the wrong member?*

Squirming children in hand, the women slowly walked to the door.

Jade brought up the rear, for good reason. Why was the woman here, so soon after the meet-up? she thought miserably. At least Brady is home. He'll know what to say to the woman. He'll know what to do.

Brady had a gift for charming women.

They all knew it. Especially Jade.

Lorna stopped before opening the door. "Listen, before we enter, I just want to say one thing. No matter who they dump, I refuse to let their decision dictate my feelings toward any of you. I like you, and I hope we'll continue to be friends."

Jade clasped Lorna's hand. They could barely hear her husky whisper. "Thanks, Lorna. I'll always remember you said that."

Jillian nodded adamantly. She was too choked up to talk, but her eyes sparkled with her tears.

Ally laughed. "Yeah, well, my sorority hazing was worse. Besides, we're all in this together, right? No matter what. That's what friends are for."

The same thought crossed each woman's mind:

Friends. That was the goal of acceptance to the club wasn't it? And I need friends in my life, now, more than ever.

Ally put out her hand. It was clasped by Jillian, then Jade, then finally, Lorna.

Now, Lorna had a reason to smile, too. "Shall we, ladies?"

—To Be Continued—

NEXT UP!

TOTLANDIA: Book 2 (The Onesies/Winter)

In this second book of the Totlandia series, five mommies are just one misstep away from entry into the elite Pacific Heights Moms & Tots Club. Everyone has a scandalous secret to hide, but who will be the next to fall? With just four spots remaining, will the five remaining ladies turn cutthroat? Or will their newfound friendships be strong enough to help them band together?

The Housewife Assassin's Greatest Hits (Book 16)

The Housewife Assassin's Fourth Estate Sale (Book 17)

The Housewife Assassin's Horrorscope (Book 18)

More Josie Brown Novels

The Candidate

Secret Lives of Husbands and Wives

The Baby Planner

HOW TO REACH JOSIE

To write Josie, go to:
mailfromjosie@gmail.com

To find out more about Josie, or to get on her eLetter list
for book launch announcements, go to her website:
www.JosieBrown.com

You can also find her at:

www.AuthorProvocateur.com

twitter.com / JosieBrownCA

facebook.com / josiebrownauthor

pinterest.com / josiebrownca

instagram.com / josiebrownnovels